LLS AND SMELLS

BELLS AND SMELLS

ANDREA FRAZER

Bells and Smells

ISBN 9781783756841

This edition publisher by Accent Press 2014

This book is dedicated to Major Jonathan Redding and Peter Needham, without whom none of these books would have been possible.

DRAMATIS PERSONAE

Feldman, Rev. Florrie – new incumbent at St Cuthbert's, Ford Hollow

Ian Brown, Mon Repos, High Street – crucifer

Burton, Albert – Tulip Cottage, Drovers Way – head chorister

Davies, Gail and Clive – licensees of The Plume of Feathers, Dairy House Lane

Garfield, Polly – the Old Bakery, Dryden's Passage – cleaner

Hartley, John – boyfriend of Chelsea Winter

Jell, Joel and Lisa – Bluebell Cottage, Drovers Way – step-father and mother of Chelsea Winter

Monaghan, Rev. Jude – The Rectory, Church Street, Carsfold – head of the Team Ministry

Mundy, Marjorie – Eyebrows, Pig Lane – an elderly wit with health problems

Pooley, Yvonne and David – Wheel Cottage, High Street – she, choir mistress and organist.

Scardifield, Willard and Thea – Clouds, Fallow Fold Road – both in the choir, he the stand-in organist

Slater, Sylvia and Silas – Vergers Cottage, Pig Lane – he the thurifer

Sutherland, Elodie – Lizanben, High Street – an elderly spinster who lives with her very old mother. Lay Reader

Winter, Chelsea – daughter of Lisa Jell

Of Market Darley Police Station

Detective Inspector Harry Falconer
Detective Sergeant 'Davey' Carmichael
Detective Constable Chris Roberts
Detective Constable Neil Tomlinson
Desk Sergeant Bob Bryant
PC Merv Green

PC John Proudfoot
Superintendent Derek 'Jelly' Chivers
Josie – server in the canteen
Vi – cook in the canteen
Associates
Dr Philip Christmas – Forensic Medical Examiner for the force
Dr Hortense 'Honey' Dubois – mental health consultant

Landbank Ltd
Trevelyan, Cardew – finances and bookkeeper
Grimble, Sheridan – architect
Smallwood, Xavier – surveyor and new land sourcing
Aylesford, Sigmund – sales and negotiations

Others
Greenslade, Michael – chief planning officer
Carstairs, Kenneth – a member of the planning committee
Dibley, Victor – a member of the planning committee

PROLOGUE

Ford Hollow wasn't a very pretty village, nor was it of any size. In fact, if it hadn't been for the presence of St Cuthbert's Church it would have been a hamlet.

In the past, its few inhabitants had relied on local farms to provide the men with agricultural work, and this had been fine – then. Now, the rivulet that cut off a corner of the River Darle had spread out, encouraged by wetter weather, and had made the rather boggy land at the south end of the farm there absolutely impossible for raising either animals or crops. The farm had floundered, and eventually the farmer and his family had moved elsewhere.

It was long after this that the farmer, now an old man, managed to offload the parcel of land on to a company which rejoiced in the name Landbank Ltd, which had then sold it on in tiny parcels to investors, in the hope that, although zoned as agricultural, it may one day become development land, as the housing shortage squeezed tighter and tighter.

There were two centres for gathering in the village: the afore-mentioned church was one, the other was the only public house, The Plume of Feathers. Both attracted a strong and faithful clientele, and the church also had a mother and toddler group, a branch of the Mothers' Union, a lot of vying for places on the cleaning and flowers rotas, a choir, and a Brownie pack.

The Plume of Feathers had a team of enthusiastic darts players, a five-a-side football team, and a cribbage team, and was well attended most nights of the week.

The only retail establishments were a shabby early sixties redevelopment of three terraced premises, offering a general store, a post office, and a fruit and vegetable retailer who tried, as far as was possible, to stock his shop from the local allotments and smallholders who were not at too far a remove.

The rest of the buildings in the village, all residential except for the church and pub, were a hotch-potch of dates and styles. There were a couple of older properties which were still thatched, and a row of farm labourers' cottagers down Drovers Way that had been bought up by a builder when they were all but derelict, had been renovated with a keen eye to price, then sold on for maximum profit, one to a local for investment, who then rented it out. There were also a few Victorian/Edwardian houses and a couple of pairs of thirties semis. No one century or decade had been able to make anything much of Ford Hollow.

As the story opens, Ford Hollow has just had a new incumbent appointed at St Cuthbert's, who will be a new member of the local team ministry, headed up by Rev. Monaghan, who lives in Carsfold and whose responsibilities cover not only Ford Hollow and Carsfold, but also the villages of Downland Haven and Coldwater Pryors, neither of which has its own vicar at the moment, and they are, therefore, served in rota form by the head of the team himself.

Chapter One

Wednesday

Reverend Florrie Feldman looked round the large, high-ceilinged sitting room with its massive windows – her favourite room in her new home – and smiled. She had been sad to leave Shepford St Bernard, but it had been a short if eventful time for her first parish, and she was looking forward to a rather smoother ride at St Cuthbert's.

This was some vicarage, she thought. It must have been built when vicars were of independent means and, consequently, could afford to keep large families. It was marvellous, though, to have so much space for meetings and events which she would host in the future. She loved the space, and wouldn't feel at all as if she was rattling around in it, with only her new cat Kelly Finn, a blue Burmese her parents had treated her to on her birthday. Her previous pet had, unfortunately, been killed by a car, and she had missed him sorely.

Kelly Finn was still in her wicker basket for travelling, as the furniture had not yet arrived and, instead of hanging around like a spare part, she decided that, now she had had a peek around the whole house, she would just nip to the church to see if it was how she remembered it when she had made an incognito visit after she was told she would be moving parishes.

This had been the bishop's idea, as he only seemed now to have comprehended that she had suffered some very unfortunate incidents in Shepford St Bernard, which had been the first parish solely in her charge since she had been ordained.

Leaving Kelly Finn howling in protest at her unexpected incarceration, Rev. Florrie almost skipped out of the vicarage and down the garden path to her new place of work. St Cuthbert's was just across Pig Lane, on the opposite corner from her new home.

It was as charming as she remembered it; small, but perfectly formed, and it had some stained glass as evidence of its age. So many churches today had had their stained-glass windows vandalised, and many of them could only afford to replace them with plain panes. Not so here, and she looked with sheer pleasure at the pattern of colours that the sun made on the uneven stone floor as it streamed through the windows.

The choir stalls were small, in scale with everything else, but they were there, resplendent before the altar. There was a light burning in the sanctuary, and the faint smell of incense pervaded the place of worship, a leftover from the last service held there.

The vestry, when located, was adequate for its needs, and everything that she could see in the building was scrupulously clean, the brasses gleaming and winking in the rays of the sun, the flowers fresh and beautifully arranged. She wasn't sure of the size of the congregation, but the buildings and its appointments were well loved and looked after by those who did attend its services.

A delicate clearing of the throat just by her left shoulder made her jump, and she turned to see a woman in her mid-forties standing behind her.

'Sorry if I startled you. Are you our new vicar?'

'Guilty as charged,' admitted Rev. Florrie, and held out her hand. 'Reverend Florence Feldman, but do call me Florrie.'

'I'm Polly Garfield from The Old Bakery in Dryden's Passage, and I've just come to check whether the flower water needs changing,' the other woman said, taking the proffered hand and shaking it. She was a fairly slim woman of average height and had shoulder-length light brown hair. Today she was wearing a sensible cotton skirt and a white T-shirt, and looked very cool and collected.

'You're a regular attender, are you?'

'Fairly regular, and I'm also in the Mother's Union and my younger daughter's in the Brownie pack.'

'So, you've got both of those have you? Tell me a bit more about the church's activities.' Rev. Florrie was curious about how much activity there was for the members of the congregation, apart from services.

'Well, we've got a choir, although it's not very big; we have house groups that meet weekly on a rota of people's homes, there's, obviously, the Parochial Church Council; there's a mothers' and toddlers' group in the small hall three mornings a week, and we have, of course, our rota of cleaners and flower providers and arrangers. We tend to have coffee and a bit of a natter at the back of the church after services.' Polly Garfield positively glowed after delivering this good news that the church was alive and well, and had a good following.

'We also occasionally arrange parish picnics and line-dancing evenings,' she added, as an afterthought.

'This is a busy parish, if you've got all that going on,' the vicar replied with an answering smile. Polly Garfield's grin grew so big at this compliment that it nearly split her face in two.

'Have you shown yourself around yet?' she asked.

'I haven't taken even a peek at the organ,' Florrie replied.

'Let me show you the way.'

'Oh, dear!' exclaimed the new vicar, as she gazed on the ancient and not very venerable instrument, as she had fired it up and was pressing a note or two here and there.

'Oh, dear, indeed,' her guide replied. 'We can keep this

place immaculate and well-loved, but there's nothing but a huge bill for repair and renovations or complete replacement we can do about that old squeezebox.'

'Have you got an appeal up and running?'

'Not yet.'

'Then it's time we got one started. Would you like to be in charge of it, Polly? It'll mean keeping a record of money collected and organising events, then extracting any relevant expenses that might have been incurred.'

Polly Garfield blushed an unlovely red at being honoured with such a responsibility and again pumped the new vicar's hand, too embarrassed and overcome for speech.

'I'm going to put a leaflet through everyone's door about a parish meeting so that we can all get to know one another, but I'll also be calling on people in their homes to introduce myself, over the next week or so.'

'That'll go down well,' replied Polly, now recovered from her speechless state. 'Some parishioners are too old and frail to attend services, and they'd really appreciate that. The old vicar used to take them communion, but Rev. Monaghan says he hasn't got time what with all his other parishes. He reckons he's far too busy.'

'I'll make the time, even if I have to knit it myself,' declared Florrie, and Polly smiled at the little joke.

'Could you knit me some, too? I could always do with an extra hour here and there.'

'If I can get the wool.'

Polly Garfield excused herself and went to check all the vases, to ascertain whether they just needed topping up, or a complete change of water, while Rev. Florrie went outside again, to see if the removal lorry had turned up with all her worldly goods. God forbid anything happened to that vehicle.

Rev. Florrie arrived back at the vicarage to find a bunch of removal men staring testily at the unanswered and unyielding front door. 'Sorry, guys,' she called, quickening her pace. 'I was just taking a quick look round my new church. I didn't mean to hold you up. Shall I put the kettle on? When I can find it?'

'That's the spirit, Rev! We made sure to pack the kettle and mugs at the very back of the van for easy access, and if we can't find the teabags, we always keep a supply in the cab.' The man who addressed her was a short and portly individual with bright carrot-coloured hair and, now she had returned to let them in, a twinkle in his eye. He looked like someone who was usually very cheerful. 'Right, you lot: get unpacking. The sooner the job's done, the sooner you can have a fag break.'

Rev. Florrie went indoors, was immediately brought the kettle and mugs, with another of the team entering the kitchen with a box containing coffee, tea, and an unopened bottle of milk, the latter described as a moving-in present. She thanked him rather prettily, and he looked a little shy and replied, 'It's just something that we always do. It helps to get the tea to us quicker,' he finished naively.

'Clever idea,' she replied. 'I'll give you a whistle when the brew's ready.'

While they were sitting on the steps drinking their tea, a tall woman, probably in her late fifties, very upright and severe-looking, came through the gate and cast a disapproving glance at the gaggle of overalled men sitting outside the door.

'Visitor for you, Miss,' called out the carroty-haired man, and Rev. Florrie showed herself at the door.

'Good morning,' she called, shooing the men away so that she could offer entrance to this forbidding woman. 'I'm Rev. Florrie. How can I help you?' she asked, holding out her hand. There would be a lot of this in the near future.

'Elodie Sutherland,' the older woman announced,

grasping Florrie's with unnecessary strength. 'I've just called round to introduce myself, as lay reader of this parish.'

'Delighted to meet you. Would you like to come in and have a cup of tea with me?'

'That's very kind of you, Rev. Feldman.' So she had taken the trouble to find out Florrie's full name. 'Perhaps I could fill you in on some of the activities of the parish, and also some of the personalities.'

'And where do you live?' Florrie had already made a note of Polly Garfield's address as soon as she had got back to her new home.

'At a house with the ghastly name of "Lizanben" on the High Street, with my aged mother. My parents were called Elizabeth and Benjamin, as you've probably already guessed, and my mother won't have the name changed because she says it reminds her of happier days when my father was alive. I can't see why she should have been happier then,' she concluded.

I can, thought Florrie, but didn't say a word.

'A very common man was my father,' the rather severe woman continued. 'When my mother passes over I shall, of course, rename it. Now, I thought you'd better know a bit about what you're up against in this parish.'

Here we go, thought Rev. Florrie. She wants to get in first before someone else says something about her.

'We do have a bit of trouble with the children during service. I don't know if you know but, after the sermon, the Sunday school joins the congregation, so that they can go up to the altar rail while the adults are taking communion, and have a blessing – just the laying on of a hand on the head and a few words said – nothing complicated.

'But they are so disturbing to the general atmosphere of the service. They fidget and whisper, and bring down the tone of the devotion that the early part of the service has. I

8

have sometimes wondered if it wouldn't be better if the vicar went through to the Sunday school at some point, and blessed them en masse. That way they wouldn't have to come into the church at all and ruin the atmosphere. What do you think?'

Rev. Florrie sat a few moments in silence, then made up her mind. 'If they never come in during a service, then how are they supposed to feel part of the congregation, let alone learn how to behave during one? It's like restaurants here in England. We never take our children to them in case they misbehave, so that when they're older of course they don't know how to, never having been trusted before.

'On the continent, children attend meals in restaurants from a very early age and, therefore, learn the code of behaviour when young. Personally, I think it's imperative that the younger members of the congregation are included in at least part of the service.'

'Hmph!' Elodie Sutherland made a disapproving noise and speared the vicar with a steely gaze. 'Do you also think it right that children too young for the Sunday school should come with their parents and whinge and cry throughout the service?'

'I think a play corner in the church would solve the problem. If there were plenty of things for them to amuse themselves with, they would be less disruptive, and better-behaved when they did go into the Sunday school, and thus better-behaved when, as members of that, they joined the service for a blessing.'

'You're quite a radical cleric, aren't you?' asked Miss Sutherland.

'Not really, but I am aware of falling attendance numbers, and I want to do anything within my power not to drive people away. If we lose the parents, we lose the children, who are the next generation of church-goers.'

'We shall have to agree to differ. Now, about the other activities that have been arranged in the past: I feel I should tell you that there have been parish picnics and line-dancing nights at which alcohol has been available.'

'What, hard liquor?'

'Not exactly *hard*, but Rev. Monaghan has provided punch for participants as part of the ticket price.'

'So that he doesn't need a licence?'

'That's right, but I don't see that there's any place in the church for alcohol.'

'What about the communion wine?' Florrie parried with a small twitch of the lips.

'Well, that is, of course, not wine any more; it is the blood of Christ.'

'For those that believe, but for all forensic purposes it is, in fact, an alcoholic beverage.' Rev. Florrie wasn't going down without a fight.

'I think that's a bit radical for an ordained member of the clergy.' Neither was Miss Sutherland.

'I'm sure we'll sort all our differences out in perfect harmony, eventually,' murmured Florrie, trying to pour oil on troubled waters.

'In that case, I'll see you at the Mothers' Union meeting in the week.'

'You have children?' asked the vicar, now definitely interested.

'Not as such, but I was made an honorary member several years ago,' replied Elodie Sutherland, blushing slightly.

'How very irregular! Now, does your mother come to church or would you like me to take communion to her at home?'

'You're starting that up again, are you?'

'Most definitely. Age and infirmity should be no barrier to taking full part in a Christian life.'

'I shouldn't bother, if I were you. She says we're all going to Hell anyway, and she stopped believing in that sort of thing years ago.'

'Well, perhaps I could just visit her for a little company.'

'You may do as you like. She's a very uncooperative woman who can be extremely difficult at times.'

As she showed her visitor out, thanking her for all the information – contumely – she had imparted, Florrie decided that she would definitely go to see Mrs Sutherland at home, if only to see what living with a very catty daughter had done to her.

The removal men had just finished bringing in her possessions and had, thankfully, put everything in the room for which it was marked, and Rev. Florrie had closed the door on them and sat down to drink a mug of tea when the doorbell rang again.

With a sigh, she rose and went to answer it, pinning a smile of welcome on her face. On the step she found a slightly dumpy woman of about forty, with a determined glint in her eye. Not another one who wants to tell me how to do my job, she hoped, and held out her hand in welcome. 'Hello. And you are?'

'Yvonne Pooley, organist and choir mistress,' she announced, giving Florrie's hand an abrupt jerk downwards, and bustled her way into the vicarage. 'I came round because I am the one who was deputised by Rev. Monaghan to keep a diary of events for you when you arrived.

'I have it all written down here,' she announced, handing over some sheets of paper. 'That's all your duties for the rest of this month, by which time you should be able to keep your own diary.'

'Thank you very much, er, *Mrs* Pooley, is it?'

'It is. My husband and I live with our two children in Wheel Cottage in the High Street, should you need any help or advice. Ask any time.'

'That's very kind of you. Would you like a cup of tea?'

'That would be very refreshing.'

'Mug, or cup and saucer?'

'Cup and saucer. I do think one should do one's bit to keep up standards, don't you?' she asked, as Florrie looked guiltily at her own over-sized mug on the table.

'Oh,' fluffed Florrie, opening a cupboard door and surveying its almost empty interior. 'For a moment I forgot that almost all my stuff is still packed. I'm afraid I only have a few mugs that the removal men separated out so that I could feed them with cups of tea. I'm so sorry. Would a mug be all right, just this once?'

'I suppose so,' said Mrs Pooley, with a superior sniff. 'It'll do, just for once.' Her face had on it an expression that clearly showed that she would have been more efficient, and sorted out a separate box for cups and saucers to accommodate visitors when she had first taken possession of the property.

'Right. Let's get down to business,' she continued imperiously. 'I shall need you to provide me with a list of hymns for Sunday by Wednesday. Choir practice is on Fridays at seven o'clock in the church. We won't expect you to attend. Anthems I choose myself and run them past you before they're sung.

'We sing at weddings for a nominal payment which I really think needs revising – only about a pound per chorister at the moment. We don't do funerals. Sometimes there are services which involve all the churches in the team ministry and, for these, we usually have a combined choir, practices for which are held in Carsfold. Again, you need not be involved.

'Unless you have a particular request, processional music and any other incidental stuff is usually chosen by me, but your views will be taken into account. Also, I hold a church key so that I can go in anytime to practise on the organ. I expect to retain this to maintain the standard of the playing. Do you have any questions?'

'No,' Rev. Florrie almost whispered. Mrs Pooley knew what she was about, and wasn't going to be diverted from her course by anyone, especially not some upstart of a female vicar.

'So, I'll see you on Sunday, then, if that's all.'

'Thank you very much for the information, Mrs Pooley. I'll make a note of everything you've told me.'

'You'll find it all in the notes I've made for you.' Yvonne Pooley rose from her chair, her mug of tea hardly touched, and marched off to the front door, where she efficiently let herself out.

Rev. Florrie remained in her chair. That had told her, hadn't it? She'd have to adhere to current practice, or she'd have a real war on her hands.

There were no more unscheduled visitors that day, so she buckled down to some unpacking, before slipping into bed, exhausted, at about half-past eleven, determined to visit some of her parishioners at home the next day.

Chapter Two

Thursday

Florrie had been given a short list of names in advance by Rev. Monaghan of people she should meet as soon as she moved in, and she consulted it now, seeing that as Miss Sutherland and Mrs Pooley had already called, she could ignore them. Still on the list were Silas Slater, the thurifer, Ian Brown, crucifer, Albert Burton who, at ninety-two, was the oldest member of the choir and nominal head chorister, and Marjorie Mundy who, her list informed her, knew everything that was going on in the parish and was, therefore, an invaluable source of information.

Looking at their addresses, she noticed that two of them actually lived in Pig Lane, so she decided to call on Silas Slater at Vergers Cottage first, then go across the road to Eyebrows to introduce herself to Marjorie Mundy. After that, she could make her way to Ian Brown at Mon Repos in the High Street, and make her final call on Albert Burton at Tulip Cottage in Drovers Way. If she made it nippy, she could be finished in time for lunch.

Silas Slater and his wife, Sylvia, were both at home as they were retired, and made her very welcome, offering her tea or coffee before she could even take a seat in their somewhat old-fashioned living room. Accepting a cup of coffee, she commented on the immaculate state of their garden, although she had only seen the front of the property on the way in.

'It keeps us out of mischief, Vicar, now neither of us is

in paid employment,' replied Sylvia.

'And it gives us a great deal of pleasure too,' added Silas.

'Have you lived here long?' Florrie asked.

'Forty years now, since we were first married,' Silas informed her, as Sylvia had disappeared into the kitchen to make coffee.

'And how long have you been thurifer?'

'About twenty years. I took over from a very old gentleman who died, and the old vicar asked me if I'd like to do it. I'm allowed to administer the host as well.' He smiled at this, as if he felt it an honour.

'And is it a happy parish?'

'In the main, although there are a few old biddies that love to gossip and cause trouble from time to time: I don't suppose we're anything special.'

Rev. Florrie learnt little from the couple. Although they were heavily involved in parish activities, they did not gossip or socialise much outside of the congregation. They had no children and very much kept themselves to themselves, although they were friendly and welcoming, and she felt comfortable in their company.

Her next call was to a thatched cottage that did, in fact, have thatching that very much resembled a pair of eyebrows round its two upstairs windows. It took a while to get an answer to her knock, but she heard a wheezy voice calling out that she'd be there soon enough.

Marjorie Mundy proved to be a short woman who was quite overweight, and who walked with two sticks. Her hair was un-styled and grey, and stood out from her head in what resembled an elderly halo.

As the woman greeted her. The vicar looked in horror at her left breast, from which a plethora of pins stuck out. 'Oh, my dear,' she said solicitously. 'Have your hurt yourself?'

This question was greeted by a wheezy chuckle as the

old woman looked down to confirm what Florrie was looking at, and she grinned at her mischievously. 'I had a mastectomy donkey's years ago,' she explained. 'I can't be doing with a prosthesis at my age, so I just shove a couple of old socks in the cup of my bra, and I tend to use it as a pincushion when I'm sewing. I'm sorry if it startled you, but I wasn't expecting visitors this morning.'

Both of them burst into laughter, and Marjorie slowly guided her guest into the sitting room, offering her the inevitable cup of tea or coffee. 'I won't, if you don't mind. I've just come from the Slaters', and I've just had a cup of coffee. I don't want to be running to the loo all day, do I?'

'That suits me fine,' replied Marjorie, slowly lowering her bulk into an easy chair where her sewing sat on a table next to it. 'So, you're the new vicar, are you? You're going to ruffle a few feathers, and no mistake.'

'Why's that?'

'Well, you're a woman, and some of those silly old women do like a male vicar to flutter their eyelashes at. You're going to put them in a right quandary. And they've made a thing of using the title Father. Since we lost our last vicar, it's been Father Monaghan this, Father Monaghan that. They'll not know what to do about you at all.'

'Perhaps there are a few dykes in the parish who can flirt with me,' replied Florrie, without thinking, and coloured up as she realised how her flippant remark may be taken, but Marjorie was having a jolly good chuckle at the thought.

'Maybe you'll bring some of those silly old dears out of the closet,' she said, stifling another chesty chuckle. 'Have you had any visitors since you arrived?'

'I have, actually – two. A woman called Sutherland and another called Pooley.'

This elicited another wheeze of amusement from her hostess, and Florrie looked at her interrogatively.

'The Sutherland woman is the perfect likeness of a sacrificial virgin. She was so angry at not being born male and, therefore, not being able to be a parish priest, that she became a lay reader. Then the church began to ordain women, but she had to stay at home and look after her frail mother.

'She's so High Church she even asks for her confession to be heard every now and again, although I don't know if she'll be so anxious to confess all to a woman. She's as close to being a Catholic as makes no difference, but she won't take the final step and convert.

'She's even wangled being made an honorary member of the Mothers' Union, and generally has a finger in every parish pie. All in all, she's a right nosy parker and a spiteful gossip to boot. I'd steer clear of getting too close to her if I were you.

'As for that Pooley woman, she's got a bee in her bonnet, at the moment, at the proposed development on the old farm land, but I don't suppose you know anything about that, being new here, do you?'

'I've no idea what you're talking about,' replied Florrie, deciding that this elderly woman could be a fount of parish knowledge, and she had a sense of humour, too, and didn't take herself too seriously.

'The last farm in the area was up at the end of Pig Lane. It farmed all the land between there and where the road curls round the other side, and its land was split by the road where the ford is. It used to be good land, but in the last few decades the stream has become boggier and boggier, and the land around it sodden and unfit for growing.

'The last farmer moved out years ago because he couldn't make a go of it any more. The buildings were in a dreadful state of repair because there was no money coming in. They're derelict now. He couldn't find anyone to buy it, so it just sat there deserted.

'Then, a while ago, along comes this company with the name of Landbank Ltd, and bought if off him for a song. He was delighted to get anything, as he thought he'd never offload it, but they immediately started to sell it on in tiny parcels to gullible folk who were willing to wait for times to get better and building land to get scarcer, so that Landbank could apply for a change of use from agricultural land to development land. It would be sold to a developer, and they'd all make a packet.

'It's madness. The houses would be at risk of flooding every time there's a spell of wet weather. Anyway, our Mrs Pooley got wind of this, and she started a petition, and then, when nobody would take any notice of her, she got a small group together to go to the headquarters of Landbank Ltd to make a personal protest.

'Now, she spends all the free time she has writing to newspapers and the Prime Minister protesting about the village being swamped in new housing, and organising meetings to plan strategy for further ways to hamper the future developers. She's obsessed. Did she mention it?'

'No.'

'Then you were lucky. She's a development bore most of the time, and I avoid her whenever I can. Thank goodness I'm not in the choir. That land may have been sold on, but I can't see the local authority approving high density housing on it. It just wouldn't be safe to live there, with the weather having gone all mad over the last couple of years, but I suppose there's no accounting for back-handers, is there?'

'What's the current situation?' asked Florrie, now intrigued.

'Nobody seems to know, not even the ever-probing Mrs Pooley. It's all gone very quiet, so maybe there are dark deeds afoot.'

Rev. Florrie suddenly became conscious of time passing and looked at her watch, exclaiming, 'I've got to get on. I've a couple more visits to make before lunch, but it's been lovely meeting you. Maybe I could come back some other time.'

'That would be nice, dear. You could bring me communion, if you wanted. I can't get to the church as regularly as I'd like to, what with this chest and my arthritis.'

'It's a deal,' agreed Florrie. 'Don't get up. I can see myself out.'

It wasn't far to Ian Brown's house in the High Street, but she could get no response from her knocks and rings at the door. On the other hand, there was no guarantee that he was retired, so he was probably at work. She'd have to call on him during an evening, or on Saturday, for she must introduce herself before the Sunday service.

Her next visit was to Drovers Way, where there was a terrace of four cottages, and in the first in the row lived Albert Burton, ninety-two years of age and still a chorister – in fact, head chorister, she had been reliably informed.

Her knock was answered by an emaciated, stringy old man with wisps of white hair on his head, his eyes a faded denim blue. He smiled at her, shook hands somewhat shakily, and invited her in. 'Would you like something?' he asked, in a quavering voice.

'No thank you. I believe you're the head of the choir,' replied Florrie.

'That's right. Sit yourself down, gal. I've been in a church choir since I was thirteen, man and boy, and I know the *English Hymnal* inside out. Give me any number, and I'll tell you what hymn it is.'

'Number 386,' she said, after a slight hesitation and, not only did he tell her the hymn, but also the tune. They did this a few times, and those that had alternative tunes listed, he could remember as well. 'That's amazing,' she declared.

'Just long familiarity,' he said, modestly. 'I know every hymn in that there book, and I've just about got the hang of that new-fangled *English Praise* as well.'

'I think that's remarkable.' Rev. Florrie was impressed. 'And what part do you sing?'

'Bass,' he replied, 'but I know all the parts by heart,' and suddenly gave her a line of 'Onward Christian Soldiers' in a voice that had not the slightest sign of a tremor, and was surprisingly strong.

'Wow!' she said. 'How long have you lived here?'

'I lived in Bristol when I were a lad, then, as soon as I was old enough, I enlisted in the army. When I got back, my mother had died, but my father had moved here to be near his sister, so this is where I settled.'

'And are you married?'

'Was, but she passed on years ago. Got one boy, but he's near retirement age and doesn't live local. I sees him about four or five times a year.'

Florrie didn't really know how to respond to a life so worn-out and filled with loss. 'You'll be at choir practice, I expect,' she said, because she couldn't think of any other reply.

'Never miss it,' Albert replied with a smile of contentment.

'I'll be off then. Lovely to have met you.'

'Be nice to have a good-looking young lass as vicar,' he replied, casually pinching her bottom as she turned to leave.

Cheeky old sod, she thought, as she bustled, somewhat embarrassed, toward the vicarage and her lunch – fancy being goosed by a ninety-two-year-old man. She hoped he didn't have designs on her virtue, such as it was.

When she got back to the vicarage, she consulted the papers that Yvonne Pooley had given her, to find that she had a PCC meeting this evening, in the vicarage itself, so she mentally cancelled her plans for the afternoon's visiting, and decided to devote herself to unpacking, as there would be teas and coffees and plates of biscuits to dispense tonight, as well as her needing a room clean and tidy enough in which to hold the meeting.

Eventually, every chair she owned was in the huge sitting room, and numerous cups and saucers were laid out in the kitchen. On the dot of seven o'clock, there was a ring at the doorbell, and she thought, I'm on: time to perform for what will probably be my biggest critics.

There were a couple of apologies due to late holidays or illness, but all the people she had already met were there, including Polly Garfield, whom she had spoken to in the church, plus a few more. Ian Brown was amongst them, and she made a point of introducing herself to him before the meeting started, and telling him that she had tried to call on him, but he must have been at work, a conclusion she came to by observing his age, which was somewhere in his thirties. His hair had greyed early, though, so it was difficult to put a more precise age on him.

He admitted to having been crucifer for the last two years, taking over the role just before the old vicar had retired, and they had had no replacement until now, so he wasn't needed every Sunday; just the ones that Rev. Monaghan deigned to hold service there.

Willard Scardifield, and Clive Davies (the landlord of The Plume of Feathers, which was a surprise) were, as yet, unknown territory. Clive told Florrie that he was just keeping an eye on the only other entertainment in town. 'Got to keep tabs on the opposition, haven't you?' he commented jovially, beery breath wreathing the vicar's head.

'Indubitably,' she replied, trying to move slightly further away.

'You must come in sometime and meet the wife. She'd

be pleased to make your acquaintance.'

'I'll definitely do that and, er, keep an eye on the competition, eh?'

'That's the spirit, Vicar. The first drink's on the house.'

'How very kind.' Moving away gratefully, she approached Willard Scardifield, whom she had not previously spoken to.

'I've been told that you're Willard Scardifield, but we've not yet met: Rev. Florrie Feldman. I'm sorry I haven't had time yet to call round and introduce myself.'

'Don't you worry, Vicar. We know you've only just moved in, so me and the wife didn't expect you. You'd be welcome anytime, though. If you come round in the evening, maybe you'd like to share a glass of wine with us?!'

'That's very kind of you,' Florrie replied, conscious that there was already alcohol on his breath, as there had been from the pub landlord, and wondering if he had a problem. There had been a gleam in his eye when he mentioned wine that was more than enthusiasm; it had been more a sort of longing.

She took the floor for the first fifteen minutes, giving them all a potted life history of how she had ended up in the church, and what had happened at her first parish, which they, no doubt, had read about in the papers at the time, then asked if there were any pressing parish matters, as it would take her a while to settle in.

As she mentioned settling in, she suddenly remembered her beloved cat Kelly Finn, still languishing in one of the spare bedrooms where she had been shut away until Florrie had completed the moving-in, and she had been operating on automatic pilot ever since, just feeding her and watering her and clearing her litter tray. She was such an undemanding cat that she hadn't even complained. She really must let her out later, or she'd think she'd been deserted, but she'd had no time to even think of her poor darling, life had been such a whirl for the last couple of days.

At this point, her attention wandered, as she was scandalised about her own infidelity to the poor animal, and she let the meeting run itself, which it had evidently been doing for some time. Decisions were made but, as she heard a sentence here and there, they didn't seem to be about anything of parish-shattering proportions and, at eight o'clock, she proposed that they should have refreshments.

When she reached the kitchen, she found Polly Garfield already there and filling cups with tea and coffee, and she hadn't even noticed her leaving the room. 'I know what everyone takes,' she explained, 'except you, so I thought it would be a good idea to get on with it.'

'Thank you so much, Polly.'

'That's no trouble. It was lovely to find everything all laid out here waiting.'

'I'll have coffee. If I fetch a couple of trays, we can take them all through together if we stack the saucers and give them out separately.'

'Good idea. I can come back for the biscuits when everyone's got a drink; give you a chance to talk to people.'

Florrie felt a prickle of apprehension run down her spine at the attention she would have on her, although this had rarely bothered her before, being part and parcel of the job. Instead of circulating as she normally would have done, she made a bee-line for Marjorie Mundy, and sat chatting to her until the meeting was called to order again by Elodie Sutherland; they dealt with AOB, then said prayers before going their separate ways.

As Rev. Florrie finally closed the door on the last of them, she wondered at her unexpected reticent reaction. Whatever could have caused that? At the moment, she had no idea, and merely hoped that it didn't happen again. It wasn't good for the image.

Kelly Finn emerged from the room where she had been incarcerated nervously, never having been in the house before, and needed some coaxing downstairs. She would be nervous for a few days to come, and Florrie wouldn't dare let her out before she had got used to her new surroundings in case she wandered off and couldn't find her way back.

Chapter Three

Friday

The next morning, Florrie locked a still-nervous cat in the kitchen, and walked down to the ford from which the village took its name to take a look at it.

In her opinion, it was getting rather big for its boots, as Marjorie had hinted, and would soon be impassable to all but four-wheel drive vehicles. That might pose a bit of a problem for access to and from Ford Hollow, and she wondered if anything was being done about it before it was too late. This was a great country for watching from the wings as problems developed, and not tackling them before they became much bigger headaches. She'd have to ask someone.

During the afternoon, she called on Marjorie Mundy again, Mrs Sutherland, and a few others who had requested or used to have home communion, keeping in mind the whole time that this evening was choir practice, and she would have to cross swords again with the indomitable and forbidding Yvonne Pooley, and run the gauntlet of Albert Burton's elderly pinching fingers.

Choir practice was scheduled for seven o'clock, so she arrived at a quarter to to open up the church, only to find that Yvonne Pooley had already done it for her, and was inside running over the accompaniment for Sunday's hymns. They had already been chosen by Rev. Monaghan, as he thought she wouldn't have time, as she only moved in on Thursday, and Mrs Pooley liked to have a list of numbers by Wednesday.

It wasn't long before choristers began dribbling in, but there weren't many of them, and Florrie decided that she would have to have a drive to recruit more members, especially if they were asked to sing at weddings. People wanted value for money these days. She was glad to note, however, that there were a couple of children who might be part of the Brownie pack, and at least one teenager. Youth was represented.

As they went through their paces, she was surprised anew at how strong Albert's singing voice remained, even when his speaking voice had weakened almost into a croak.

Everything went without a hitch, until Mrs Pooley handed out sheets of music and told them that they were to do a new anthem and the seven-fold amen, which they would perform at harvest festival, which wasn't really that far away, and there were groans from the choir stalls.

'Don't be so negative,' Yvonne exhorted them. 'I shall go over each of your parts individually, so that you can get a feel for them, then we'll just have a tentative try at putting them together.' This was greeted by even louder groans which she ignored and returned to her seat at the organ. 'We'll start with the soprano part for the anthem.'

Elodie Sutherland was bleating along with the other women in a shrill and slightly out-of-tune voice in the back row. Unfortunately, for balance, there was only one alto, and the poor woman had to sing through her part on her own – though she was fairly accurate, and could obviously read music; more than could be said for some of the others, who would have to learn it by rote. There was only old Albert singing bass, and two rather weak tenors for the lower register.

After a disastrous attempt to put all the parts together, Yvonne Pooley let out an audible sigh, and announced that they were going to try the seven-fold amen, at which point,

Albert could be heard to croak that he'd known it since he were a young 'un.

Several heads turned in his direction, giving him evil looks. There didn't seem to be anything he didn't know in the church music repertoire, but that was only because he'd been involved in the music side of it for so long. In fact, Florrie had been told by someone that he had a special medal from the Royal School of Church Music for his long service, and there weren't many who could boast that.

At last the practice drew to a close, and Yvonne rushed from her seat at the organ to announce that she had to get home to wait for a very important phone call, but would pop back later to lock up, if that was all right with everyone. She didn't want to rush anybody, and was quite happy to do this. There was a murmur of agreement, and she shot through the door like a whippet from the trap.

Rev. Florrie left with the bulk of the others, sure that Yvonne Pooley would see that everything was closed down as far as the organ was concerned, and that the place was secured when she returned. Kelly Finn wasn't quite so nervous when she got back to the vicarage, and Florrie felt that she could call the rest of the evening her own.

An hour later, a lone figure could be seen making its way to the church. This was one of the younger members of the soprano section of the choir. Sixteen-year-old Chelsea Winter had managed to leave her new sheet music behind, and needed it to practise at home. She was one of those who could read music, and she had planned to go over her part on the keyboard later that evening. Somebody had to do it right to lead the others, and she had decided, with the lack of competition from the other members of the section, that this would be her. Her mother and stepfather were well away with the booze, which was quite normal, and she needed something to do, as they were no company when they were in their cups, and would probably go off to the pub later on.

The door was still unlocked when she got back, for which she was grateful. She thought that old Pooley might have had her phone call and got everything already locked up, but she was able to slip in unobtrusively. The only light was that in the sanctuary, but there was light coming through the windows, so she didn't feel it was necessary to turn on any electric ones and draw attention to her presence.

Quietly she slipped up the aisle, her attention locked on where she had sat, and where she could see the paler patch that denoted the sheets of music that she had accidentally left there. Picking these up, she tuned round, and her eyes caught sight of someone still on the men's side of the stalls. It looked like old Albert.

'Hello, Mr Burton,' she called. 'I've just come back because I forgot my music after practice.'

Instead of the croaky reply she had expected, there was just silence, which seemed to get louder and louder. Perhaps he had been taken ill, she thought, crossing over to the other side of the stalls to check. He was very ancient, after all.

'Are you all right, Mr Burton?' she quavered. 'Are you ill?' she asked, as the silence echoed even louder in her head, and her ears began to buzz.

There seemed to be something wrong with the old man's head. Was he looking sideways and downwards? He certainly didn't look all right. Neither did he move as she approached. When she reached him, she held out a hand to touch his cheek, and still he was quiet and unmoving. Suddenly, she understood why.

The windows were open in the vicarage and, as the church was right next door, Rev. Florrie was able to hear, very faintly, the sound of someone screaming. Getting off the sofa immediately, she headed for the door and out towards the church, as the sound grew louder and louder. The door was still unlocked and, inside, she found Chelsea Winter standing in front of the altar and facing the men's side of the choir stalls, her mouth wide open, her head in her hands. She looked just like a well-known painting by Edvard Munch, but with volume.

Florrie rushed towards her, turning on lights as she advanced. When she reached the distressed girl, she put her arms around and tried to quieten her. As reply, Chelsea raised a hand and pointed towards the choir stalls she was facing, pointing out the earthly remains of Albert Burton, head chorister and ninety-two years old, now departed this life in a place where he had spent so much of his free time over the years.

Rev. Florrie pulled Chelsea's unresisting body into the vestry and pushed her down on a hard wooden chair. The screaming had stopped at last, to be replaced by a pathetic whimpering. 'What happened?' she asked, and waited for the young girl to compose herself.

'I'd forgotten my new music from practice,' she finally was able to explain. 'I crept in and found the sheets, then I noticed Mr Burton. I thought at first he'd been taken ill. Then I went over to see how he was, and found ...' She tailed off into sobbing, before adding, 'It was his head. It was all wrong, and I didn't know what was wrong, but I knew he had died.'

Florrie hugged her to her body. She was such a young thing, and this must have been a terrible shock to her. 'Are your parents at home?' she asked.

'My mother and stepfather will probably be at the pub by now, and they won't come home till closing time, bladdered as usual,' the young girl told her without a morsel of self-pity. 'That's what they do.'

The vicar pondered this unexpected information, then asked, 'Do you know a woman called Mrs Mundy?'

'The old fat lady?' asked Chelsea, without an ounce of self-consciousness.

'That's right. Lives in a house called Eyebrows. Well, I'm going to phone the police on my mobile, then I'm going to take you there while I wait for them. I'll phone the pub as well, and tell them to let your mother know you're staying over at the vicarage tonight, if that's all right with you.'

'Thank you.' Chelsea was calmer now, and this pragmatic decision seemed to please her. 'I'd like that.'

'Come on. I'm sure this crime scene will be all right for a few minutes, and I'll collect my mobile on the way back. You just wait with Mrs Mundy, and I'll call for you later but, I warn you now, I'll probably have the police in tow to take a statement from you, so be prepared.'

Marjorie Mundy was only too happy to give the girl sanctuary, knowing what her mother and stepfather were like, and applauding silently Florrie's decision to let the girl stay the night with her. 'You run along and inform the police. We'll be fine until you come back,' she said, sending her on her way.

Spending only as much time as it took her to grab her mobile phone, Florrie returned to the scene of the crime to inform the forces of law and order. Having done so, she began to search both her own and the choir's vestries, and any other dark corner nearby, to make sure that no one was hiding on the premises, and that she really was alone with a dead body.

In Market Darley police station, Detective Inspector Falconer had drawn the short straw for the rota, and was on Friday night duty. His sergeant was not on duty, and DC Roberts was on a callout when the message came through that there was a stiff in the church at Ford Hollow. Asking Bob Bryant the desk sergeant to alert Carmichael that he was needed, Falconer grabbed his phone and car keys and headed off to the car park.

He and his sergeant had been partners now for over two years, 'Davey' Carmichael – real name, Ralph Orsino – being a lowly uniformed PC when they had first been paired together. Carmichael had swiftly been moved to CID, and then received promotion to sergeant. He had married a widow with two children whom he had met on their first case together, and they had one child of their own, and his wife, Kerry, was now expecting twins. With the added presence of two little dogs, their household was about to become very chaotic indeed. The only criticism Harry Falconer had of his sergeant was of his disturbing bent towards weird and wonderful clothing, a constant source of embarrassment to the senior officer in the past.

Harry Falconer, on the other hand, was a bit of a lone body. In his early forties and with an army career already behind him, he lived in Market Darley and had had one cat when they first worked together but, as a result of an unexpectedly soft heart where the feline species was concerned, he now had five, and had promised himself that he wouldn't be duped into taking in any more. He did have a sort-of girlfriend, in Heather Antrobus, who was a nurse at the hospital in Market Darley, but it was nothing serious, and he was determined to keep things that way.

He had a horror of sharing his living accommodation with anyone else, and he had no desire to disturb the status quo. They merely shared a meal together in a little Italian restaurant, once a fortnight, and he had managed to resist her previous requests to let her come round and cook Sunday lunch for him in his own home. The furthest he had gone was to let her in for a coffee sometimes after they had eaten out.

When he pulled up outside the church in Ford Hollow, he wasn't surprised to see Carmichael's car already parked there, as Castle Farthing, where the sergeant lived, was much closer to Ford Hollow than Market Darley. The man was still driving the disgraceful old Skoda that he had owned when they first became partners, whereas Falconer had a Boxster which he was already thinking of trading in for something a little newer, but still as sporty. After all, who did he have to spend his money on other than himself? Life was just the once, so you had to make the best of what you had, didn't you?

Inside, where the lights now blazed, he found his sergeant sitting in a pew with a woman in clerical garb and, when Carmichael stood up, he was horrified to see the man's knees. Was he wearing shorts on an official call-out?

No, not Carmichael. He had gone one better and was actually wearing a bang up-to-date black kilt, the like of which could not possibly have been seen in Market Darley, let alone the villages. Falconer thanked the good Lord that he wasn't sporting a sporran as well, and approached him with a disapproving expression on his face, and wondering why the woman looked familiar.

On being introduced to Rev. Florrie, he remembered at once where they had met before, on a case in the village of Shepford St Bernard, and asked her if she had jumped from the frying pan into the fire, as she had evidently been moved to a different parish.

'It certainly looks like it, doesn't it?' she commented. She smiled at him and shook hands, having enjoyed, as much as she could considering the circumstances, her contact with the pair in the past, and she liked and respected them, now feeling certain that this matter would be cleared up satisfactorily, and the right person punished for what they had done. Justice would be done by old Albert. Suddenly, she felt tears pricking her eyes and looked away.

'Sit yourself down, Rev. Florrie, compose yourself, then tell me what has happened here,' said Falconer in a soft voice. Without replying, she pointed up to the choir stalls, and took a handkerchief out of her pocket.

Both policemen looked in that direction, and started off towards the stalls to take a look. Albert Burton looked at peace where he sat, the only discordant note being the angle of his head. It looked to both of them as if someone had broken his neck. What a bizarre thing to happen in a country church, thought Falconer, and then corrected himself. In his experience in and around the villages, anything could and had happened.

Moving back towards the vicar still sitting in a pew, he asked, 'Was it you who found him like this?'

'No, it was one of the younger members of the choir who had left her new music behind by accident. She's only about sixteen.'

'Where is she now?'

'She's with an elderly neighbour. She told me that both her mother and her stepfather would be in the pub till closing time, being regular drinkers, and I told her I would phone the pub and get the landlord to pass a message on to her mother that she would be spending the night at the vicarage – which I did straight away. She didn't seem to be too bothered. I hope I didn't do wrong.' She looked at him pleadingly, wondering if she should have kept Chelsea in the church, but that had seemed too cruel with Albert's rapidly cooling body still present. It was mid-September, and the evening temperature dropped quickly now.

'We couldn't have done better ourselves,' replied Falconer, patting her hand as she looked at him unsurely.

'I did tell her I would probably bring you back with me to take a statement, so she knows she'll be interviewed tonight.'

'Good girl. At least you got her away from the horror she must have felt when she found the body. Why did you come into the church?'

'I could hear her screams from the vicarage. It's only across the road, so I rushed over to see what on earth was happening, and found the poor soul standing between the two sets of choir stalls, just like Munch's *The Scream*, with her head in her hands. She was hysterical with shock, so I thought a dose of Marjorie Mundy's very pragmatic outlook on life would be just what she needed – somebody steadying and not prone to over-reacting.'

'You did just the right thing. If you'll excuse me a minute while I phone for transport for your late chorister, and a SOCO team, you can tell us as much as you know.' With that, Falconer went to the back of the church to make his call, while Rev. Florrie enquired after Carmichael's family, delighted to know that there would be two new additions to it next spring.

Returning to them after a couple of minutes, he said, 'I presume he was a chorister, judging by where he was found. Am I right?'

'He was head chorister. He told me when I went round to his house that he'd lived here since just after the war, and had been in church choirs since he was thirteen, and he is … was ninety-two.' She gulped, as she acknowledged her use of the past tense. 'I still can't believe he's dead.'

'Where did he live, Florrie?'

'In Tulip Cottage in Drovers Way. He lived all on his own, poor old man, but he didn't seem at all downhearted.'

'Well that's the way to be really, isn't it?' declared Carmichael, suddenly demonstrating maturity beyond that of someone who would wear a kilt to visit a church. 'There's no point in going round miserable all the time. That's just letting your life go to waste.'

'Well said, Sergeant,' agreed Falconer, and smiled at the vicar with encouragement. 'Chin up, Reverend. He was a lucky man to get to that age. He could've lost his life in the war, like so many others.'

'That's true, but it's so unfair that someone just snuffed out that spark of life and vitality that he had. He just loved his church music, and knew the *English Hymnal* back to front. There wasn't any number he couldn't identify, with alternative tunes listed as well.'

'Then we'll just have to hope that he's joined the heavenly chorus, and is singing with them now, won't we,' said Carmichael, gently. He was turning out to be a really thoughtful policeman, and Falconer acknowledged his apt remark with a glance of approval, and a mental note to speak to him severely about his flawed sense of what it was appropriate to wear to a crime scene – again.

When they had handed over the crime scene, they went round to Marjorie Mundy's cottage and collected Chelsea, taking her back to the vicarage to make her meagre statement, then they left her for Rev. Florrie to comfort and tuck up in bed with a hot drink.

After they left the vicarage, Falconer suggested that they ought to try the pub, to see if they could at least inform Chelsea's parents that she was safe and sound. The Plume of Feathers was alive with life and noise, this being Friday night, and they had to push their way through the crowd to attract the landlord's attention.

They had passed Clive Davies outside, smoking, so knew that it was Gail they would find on duty behind the bar. When she was free from serving, she came and asked what she could get them. 'Oh, we don't want a drink,' explained Falconer, showing her his warrant card. 'We'd like to speak to Chelsea Winter's parents, if they're in here, which we believe they are.'

'Over there by the fireplace,' replied Gail. 'Has something happened to Chelsea?' she asked, looking worried.

'Nothing. We just need to have a word with them.'

'Their names are Joel and Lisa Jell. Chelsea's got a different surname because she's from Lisa's first marriage,' Gail informed them, saving them a minute or so when speaking to the girl's parents.

Falconer broke in on what appeared to be the early

stages of an argument. 'Excuse me, but are you Mr and Mrs Jell?'

'What of it?' queried Joel, rather aggressively. He'd sunk quite a few that night, and was feeling a fight, or at the very least, a shouting match, coming on.

'Mrs Jell, do you have a daughter called Chelsea?' the inspector continued.

'Omigod! What's happened to our Chelsea? Is she hurt? Dead? Raped?'

'Calm down, Mrs Jell. Nothing's happened to her. I just need to tell you something.'

'What's she done? If it's boys, or she's been shoplifting again, I'll skin her alive.'

'Mrs Jell, will you just listen, please. Chelsea has witnessed something rather upsetting tonight, and I've taken her to the vicarage to stay, as she's had something of a shock.'

'You're not going to take my little girl away from me. I am a good mother. I just have to get out of the house, sometimes …' Her eyes rolled as testament to how much alcohol she had imbibed.

'Nobody's trying to take her away. Let's get you and your husband home, and we'll explain exactly what has happened.'

'But it ain't closing time yet,' she protested.

'Don't worry, love,' growled her husband, leaning over and putting an unsteady arm round her. 'There's a big bottle of wine in the fridge, so we won't go thirsty.'

'That's all right, then,' she agreed, and immediately looked more cheerful.

The couple travelled from the pub to Drovers Way in Carmichael's car, as Falconer was unwilling to have anyone throw up in his Boxster, especially as he was thinking of trading up. The smell of sick was hell to get rid of, and, as he explained to Carmichael, as a family man, he often had sick or under the weather children in his car, so it wouldn't be such a tragedy, as he was probably used to it.

Back at the cottage, Joel went immediately towards the tiny kitchen to fetch the wine from the fridge, and Lisa threw herself full-length on the sofa, having extracted a half-bottle of vodka from her capacious handbag and taken a hearty slug. 'So, wha's goin' on with our Chelsea, then?' she demanded, beginning to sound slightly slurry.

Carmichael took out his notebook and perched on the arm of a chair in the minuscule sitting room, while Falconer took a seat in the chair itself. 'It would seem that your daughter left her new music behind after choir practice.'

'Fluff-brained little cow.'

Ignoring this casually insulting remark, Falconer continued, 'When she got back to the church, she had the misfortune to find Mr Albert Burton dead in the choir stalls.'

'What? That churchy old git that lives next door?'

'Does he really? Or rather, did he?'

'Yes. I hope you're not implying that his death had anything to do with our Chelsea. Why, she'd never hurt a fly!'

'Nothing whatsoever, Mrs Jell, although Mr Burton was murdered. She was so shocked and upset that the vicar took her back to the vicarage for the night, and asked that you be informed.'

'The interfering bitch. Is she implying that I'm not fit to be a mother?'

'Nothing of the sort. She just thought that your daughter might need some time to compose herself. Do you know the vicar?' asked the inspector.

'Not as such, although we do occasionally pop into the church of a Sunday, don't we, Joel?'

'Not that much, and I'd heard tell that there was some new woman vicar,' mumbled her husband, from the depths of his wine glass. 'Shouldn't be allowed, if you ask me. Woman's place is in the kitchen.'

'But your daughter's a member of the church choir,' said Carmichael, a slightly interrogative tone to his statement.

'Anything to be different from us,' replied Lisa Jell, necking her full glass of wine. 'She's at that sort of rebellious age.'

And doing it back to front, thought Falconer, as the unsavoury couple poured wine down their throats like they were dying of thirst. Usually teenagers drink too much, and experiment with drugs and sex. This one's going off the rails by going to church, because her primary carers are so badly behaved. He'd have to ask around about these two.

Mrs Jell had now reached the point of incoherence and, pouring the dregs of the wine into his own glass, Joel asked the two detectives if they could give Lisa a hand upstairs as, if he tried, they'd probably both fall down and break their necks, and Falconer wondered how many times Chelsea had performed this task. No wonder she attended church. She probably felt she needed all the help she could get from on high.

Falconer went up backwards, holding her hands, and Carmichael went up behind her, his hands at her waist to steady her if she started to lose her balance, but it wasn't an easy task. She was like an inebriated octopus – all legs – and mouthy with it.

They finally got her sitting on her bed, where she fell back, passed out. Carmichael took her legs, with a distasteful expression on his face, and lifted them on to the bed, while Falconer took off her shoes. 'That looks to be all we can do for tonight,' said the inspector, and they left Joel Jell downstairs, finishing the last of the wine and softly singing to himself.

'What a couple. Poor Chelsea,' were Carmichael's only

words, before Falconer launched into him.

'What the hell do you think you're doing, coming out to a crime scene dressed in girls' clothes?' he asked, referring to Carmichael's unconventional wearing of a kilt. 'As your superior officer, I shall be the laughing stock of the village once this gets around.'

'But they're absolutely the cutting edge of male fashion now, sir,' replied Carmichael, in his own defence.

'I don't care if they're the cutting edge of a carving knife, I will not have any of my officers dressed like women, unless they biologically are. Do you hear me? There's absolutely no precedent for men in the force wearing skirts.'

'No, but there is a fairly good historical one,' parried the sergeant.

'And what may that be, pray?'

'Jesus wore a dress.'

The end of this conversation was never recorded for the sake of decency. They headed back to the church to see what Doc Christmas thought of this most recent murder, and how the SOCO team was getting on with its evidence-gathering. The doc really loved a good murder, and relished a post-mortem the way children relished a trip to the zoo: as a real treat to be savoured.

Chapter Four

Saturday Morning

Both detectives turned up for duty the next morning, Falconer giving the forensic medical examiner, Dr Philip Christmas a ring at about ten o'clock. They knew he couldn't resist a corpse, and would come in on Doomsday if he thought he'd get to do a post-mortem. And they were right.

'I haven't had time to do the cutting and shutting, but from a preliminary examination, I'd say it was fairly obvious that he died from someone breaking his neck. It wouldn't have been too difficult a job. At his age, there'd be some degree of bone degeneration, judging from his height. Time of death somewhere between seven and ten last night. I'll give you a ring when I've finished, before I regularise things with a written report, OK?'

'Thanks a lot, Philip,' said Falconer with genuine appreciation, and finished the call, immediately turning to Carmichael and asking, 'Where's Roberts this morning? I thought he was on duty.'

'Dunno, sir. Maybe he switched shifts with someone,' replied the sergeant, not very much bothered, as the detective constable was so often absent with illness or injury. Shall I ring down and ask Bob Bryant?'

'Don't bother. I'll leave a note for him, and we'll slope off to the morgue and pick up the old man's house keys. I doubt they'd have been transferred to the station last night. Might as well have a look around it first, don't you think?

Before they could leave the office however, Falconer's telephone rang, and he answered it to find DC Chris Roberts on the line. 'Where the hell are you, Roberts?' he bellowed. They'd never got on very well, as Roberts was a bit workshy, and could, more often than not, be found either with his feet up on his desk reading the newspaper or out in the car park, having a crafty smoke and, if he wasn't engaged in either of these two activities, he was probably on sick leave.

'I'm at home, sir. Waiting for the police,' he replied, his voice somewhat tight.

'All you had to do was to come in here, and there are loads of them,' came back at him, rather sarcastically.

'I can't, sir.' There was a brief silence, then Roberts went on, 'The thing is, I've been burgled, and there's been some vandalism. I'm waiting now for someone to come and check for fingerprints and take photographs.'

Falconer gave a huge sigh of resignation, and asked what had happened. 'I don't know whether they happened at the same time or separately, but I came down this morning to have breakfast, then I went up to get showered and dressed. I'd shooed a cat off the garden when I first came down and I must have forgotten to lock the back door.

'When I was in the shower, I heard something being knocked over – you know how little you can hear over the sound of the water,' – especially when you're singing, Roberts thought silently. 'By the time I'd got out and wrapped a towel round me, I heard the front door slam, and whoever it was, was gone.'

'You're a policeman. How on earth could you have been so stupid as to have gone into the shower leaving the back door unlocked? Did you learn nothing in training?'

'This is a very quiet and respectable neighbourhood, but I think whoever it was knew what I do for a living. When I eventually got a look out of the front door, I noticed that someone had sprayed graffiti on it. There was the word "pig" and a very crude outline of the animal. Whether that was done during the hours of darkness or this morning, I have no idea.'

'Roberts, you're a disaster waiting to happen. You've hardly been back any time since you had mumps, and now you're stuck at home after being turned over.'

'I know, sir, and I'm sick of it too. I'm beginning to think I shouldn't have got transferred back here or, at least, not made it permanent.'

This elicited only a period of silence, followed by, 'Come in when you're able to. If we're not here, either ask Bob Bryant whether anything new has come in, or give one or other of us a ring on our mobiles, OK?'

'Okey-dokey, guv … I mean, sir.'

Falconer's expression was sour with disapproval as they left the office, Carmichael, silent, as he had got the gist, at least, of the fact that they wouldn't see DC Roberts any time soon.

'Can I stay in the car, sir?' asked Carmichael when they arrived at the mortuary. He had a notoriously weak stomach, and had thrown up on numerous occasions during their time working together.

'Do you want me to get you crisps and a soft drink?'

'Aw, sir, don't make fun of me. I can't help it, can I?'

'I suppose not, you great softie.'

Once in the autopsy room, Falconer was surprised by how un-human the old man looked. There was so little of him that he was more like an anatomical figure fashioned from plastic. It seemed hard to believe that this bag of bones was walking around only the day before, and had participated in choir practise just yesterday evening.

Doc Christmas directed him to where he could locate the keys, having foreseen this visit and left them on his desk, and turned back to what he was doing, his hands deep in the body cavity of the deceased, a look of quiet professional contentment on his face. He really loved this part of his work, and had been involved with Falconer and Carmichael's cases since the beginning of their partnership.

Falconer heard the pathologist whistling quietly as he exited the building and headed for the car, where Carmichael was waiting. 'Did you get them?'

'No bother. So let's get off and see if there are any clues to the old man's death in his cottage.'

Albert Burton's home was, indeed, next door to that of the Jells, they noted when they arrived, and the terrace was of very 'bijou' dwelling places. Albert probably lived here because he was on his own. Maybe the Jells lived here because they spent all their money on drink, for it was understood by everyone that the houses were rented, not owned by those who lived there.

The inside of Bluebell Cottage was what they would have expected of a very old man's home, very cluttered, with everything old and nearly worn out. The only thing not of venerable age was a set of three hard-backed hymnbooks on the sideboard which, after a quick look inside the flyleaf, turned out to have been published within the last few years.

'He was keen on his hymns, wasn't he sir?' asked Carmichael, leafing through volume one. 'These must have cost a fair bit.'

'Those books must have cost a small fortune but, if you look around here, what else did the old man have to spend it on but the one remaining passion in his life? There's a bookcase over there,' said Falconer, pointing to the far side of the little room, 'that's absolutely stuffed with various hymn books, and another, on the other side of the room, filled with books of anthems and choral works of religion.'

'And he wasn't attacked here, or his home broken into, so he couldn't have been killed for anything he possessed,' opined Carmichael, still holding the new book in his hand. 'These were published a few years ago, but it doesn't look as if they've ever been opened.'

Going into the tiny kitchen, Falconer looked in the waste bin and, under the remains of Albert's tea from the night before, but there was nothing of interest to them. 'He'd probably been saving for them since they were printed. I doubt he had very much pension, and the cost of living hasn't gone down to my knowledge. I think these were his fairly new treat and, I don't doubt that he spent the best part of his weekends looking through his treasures, looking for something he could suggest they sing in the church …' Falconer's voice weakened and finally broke off. If Carmichael had have thought it possible, he would have surmised that the inspector was trying to stop himself from weeping.

It was certainly a poignant thought, that such an elderly person with nothing else in his life should have saved for ages to buy something that would feed his passion, then have his life choked off before he had had the chance to really examine what he had waited so long for and finally bought, and Carmichael felt his own eyes sting with emotion.

'Come on,' urged the inspector, recovering himself, 'we'll find nothing here. We'll let the forensic boys go over it, and we'll get ourselves off to Rev. Florrie's and ask her who she thinks we ought to talk to first.'

It wasn't far to the vicarage, and Florrie was up, breakfasted, and in her clerical gear prior to going out. As the door opened, a blue-grey cat began to wind itself round Falconer's ankles, and he bent to stroke it. 'New member of the family?' he asked.

'Birthday present from my parents. Named Kelly Finn. My old cat … well, I don't want to talk about it, so I'll just say that there was this car, and it didn't stop.'

'I'm so sorry. I won't mention the matter again.'

'Come on in. How's life treating you, Davey?' she asked. There had scant time for polite small talk the previous evening.

'We're expecting twins next year,' he informed, with a big sloppy grin on his face.

'Congratulations. You will be a busy couple,' she replied. He had mentioned it the night before, but probably didn't remember.

'I notice you're in your work clothes. Are we disturbing you?' asked Falconer.

'Not at all. A Miss Sutherland has asked me to call round this morning, but I don't have to be there until eleven, so I've got time to make you both a drink. Tea or coffee?'

Taking a seat at her kitchen table, Falconer told them their purpose in calling round. 'I don't actually know that many people yet, as I only moved here on Thursday,' she replied, 'but if I direct you to Marjorie Mundy's house, I think she's the heartbeat of the village, or at least, the spider at the centre of its web. She can't get out much, but she keeps her ear to the ground – not literally – and everyone seems to keep her informed about what's going on.'

While they drank their coffee, Carmichael's with his usual six spoonfuls of sugar, she told them about those she had met in the parish. At the end of her little speech, Carmichael asked, 'What's a thurifer? And what's a crucifer?'

Florrie smiled at him and explained. 'The thurifer is the one who swings the thurible. Stop! I know you're going to ask me what a thurible is, and I'm going to tell you. It's a metal incense holder on chains. The incense is lit before all the people taking part in the service, like the vicar and choir, process down the aisle. The thurifer then swings the thurible, and wafts the smoke about for everyone to smell.

'The crucifer is much easier to explain. At the front of the procession down the aisle, there's a man with a big brass cross on a long stick. It is of course the Christian symbol, and he carries it ahead of everyone else. Then, at the end of the service, everyone goes out, with the crucifer at the head, and in the same order they went in.'

'Gotcha,' said Carmichael, now pleased that he wasn't being shut out by words he didn't understand, being a 'Low Church' attendee when he occasionally went to services, and Falconer made a tiny smile in Florrie's direction. She had explained it without embarrassing the man about his lack of knowledge but, who, nowadays, went to church at all, let alone High Church?

'Go and see Mrs Mundy,' she advised them, 'and remember what I said about Mr and Mrs Jell. Polly Garfield, the person I met when I first visited the church, is a very nice woman, and I should think she knows what's what around here, too. Marjorie will give you her address.'

Marjorie Mundy was still engaged in needlework that morning. When they had got Carmichael inside and given him a glass of water, and Marjorie had explained that it was just a pair of old socks the pins were stuck into (for the detectives had met with the same bosomy spectacle as had Rev. Florrie), Falconer got down to business.

'We want to speak to you about the good folks of this parish,' he began. 'I understand that you don't get out much, but that you know everyone. Usually I would get a list of people to talk to from the vicar, But Rev. Feldman has only just arrived here, and she recommended that we speak to you.'

'Sensible woman, she seems. Let me see – is your young man all right, by the way?'

'He's perfectly all right now that he knows you're not into body piercing,' replied the inspector, and Carmichael gave the ghost of a smile.

'You could speak to all the people who hold a position in the church – the thurifer, crucifer, and the choir mistress. Have you met the Jells: the parents of that young girl who found the body?'

'Unfortunately, yes.'

'Nuff said, Inspector. Well, I think you should talk to Silvia and Silas Slater, because he's the thurifer – Vergers Cottage, Pig Lane – in fact, just next door to the church, dead opposite here. Right, just let me get my head around the most logical way to make these visits.'

She thought for a moment. 'Yes, I've got it. If you want to speak to Polly Garfield, who's quite a nosy woman, she's down Dryden's passage at the Old Bakery, then Yvonne Pooley, the choir mistress. The next three take you back to the High Street, as she's at Wheel Cottage. Next should be crucifer, Ian Brown at Mon Repos, then that acid bitch Elodie Sutherland and her dried-up old stick of a mother.

'Then, if you go into Fallow Fold Road, Willard and Thea Scardifield are at Clouds. She's in the MU and the choir, he's on the PCC and fills in if they need an organist. Finally, there are Gail and Clive Davies who run the local pub. They're always at home. That should do you for now, but don't hesitate to come back if you need any more information or names.'

'Got all that, Carmichael?' asked Falconer, hopefully.

'Just about, sir.'

'Are you feeling better now, young man?'

'Yes, thank you, Mrs Mundy. It was just all those pins. I couldn't believe that someone like you would have gone in for body piercing in such an enthusiastic way.'

'I'm sorry if I upset you. I don't think about it when I'm sewing. I had the thing off about thirty years ago, and it's become second nature. It really turned the milkman's stomach once, when we had a new one, but I usually manage to remember to take them out if I'm not expecting anybody in particular.'

'Never you mind, Mrs Mundy. DS Carmichael here's fine now, aren't you, Sergeant?'

'I'm all right, sir; perfectly OK, Mrs Mundy. As I said, it was just the shock,' he replied a little shamefacedly.

'Don't worry about it, young man. If you need to come back here again you'll be forewarned, won't you. At my age, my memory isn't what it was. If you're going to Polly Garfield's first as I recommended, turn right on to the High Street at the end of Pig Lane, take the first left, and the Old Bakery is the second house on the right. Good luck.'

'Thank you very much, Mrs Mundy. You've been most helpful,' said Falconer, in farewell. 'And if we're lucky, everybody will be at home as it's Saturday,' he carried on to Carmichael. 'And if they're out shopping or something, we've got enough people to see to come back to them later.'

'And if you fancy a bite of lunch, we could go back to Castle Farthing?'

'We could always get a bite at The Fisherman's Flies, and I could just pop over and see Kerry.'

'Don't be silly. She'll feel hurt if I don't go over,' replied Falconer, looking worried. 'It's all right, Sergeant; we'll eat at the pub, then go over to have a cup of tea with her afterwards.'

'Excellent.' This plan was perfectly acceptable to Carmichael. Kerry wouldn't have to go to any trouble, as he could make the tea, and she wouldn't have felt left out of their visit to the village, as someone was bound to see them and tell her.

Chapter Five

Still Saturday morning

Vergers Cottage was only a few steps away, and the door was opened by a woman with curly grey hair, wearing a dress made of what Carmichael, at least, recognised as good old-fashioned Crimplene, which had been a favourite of his grandmother's.

'Mrs Slater,' Falconer greeted her, adding 'Detective Inspector Falconer and Detective Sergeant Carmichael of the Market Darley CID,' as they held out their warrant cards.

'You must be here about poor old Albert. What a dreadful thing that was. We can't think who would do something so dreadful to a harmless old man like that. Do come in and have a cup of tea and meet Silas, my husband. He's the thurifer, you know. We're both very involved with the church and always have been.'

She led them into a comfortably furnished sitting room and disappeared into the kitchen, where they could hear her speaking to a man with a very deep voice. As they waited for her to brew tea, the owner of the voice came in to greet them, and wasn't at all how he had sounded when he was just a voice.

Instead of a very tall, slim man with a tan and a brighter than white smile, a short, tubby man entered, his hair absolutely white, and brushed back slick, evidently dressed with some sort of pomade or other. They stood to shake hands, and he directed them back into their chairs. 'Won't be a minute with your tea. Sylvia says you're here about old Albert. Poor sod – never did anyone any harm, and always had a pleasant word if you bumped into him in the street. Have you any idea who's responsible, yet?'

'It's early days, Mr Slater,' replied Falconer, whereupon Mrs Slater entered the room with a loaded tray.

'Call us Sylvia and Silas. Everyone else does. Mr and Mrs is so formal nowadays, don't you find?'

'Agreed. OK, Sylvia, Silas, can you think of anybody who would want to do Mr Burton any harm?'

'Nobody would want to hurt him,' said Sylvia, passing round cups, followed by the sugar bowl.

'He was in his nineties. What sort of trouble could a man of that age cause?' asked Silas. 'And anyway, his only interest was church music. That's hardly a subject for fighting to the death over, now is it?'

'Were either of you at the church on Friday night?' the inspector asked, watching Carmichael, who was trying to balance a cup on one knee while he took notes on the other one. It was quite amusing.

'Not needed,' boomed Silas in his *basso profundo*. 'I'm only there of a Sunday to swing the incense. Sylvia goes to MU meetings but, apart from Sundays, that's our lot.'

'You have children?' This was not an unreasonable question as Sylvia attended Mothers' Union meetings, and the clue was on the title of this group.

'Well, no, actually. We have a lot of nieces and nephews, but God didn't bless us with any of our own.'

'Yet you go to MU meetings?'

'What? Oh, that. That Elodie Sutherland managed to worm her way in for a while, so I asked if I could attend too. At least I have some contact with children, what with our extended family, not like that shrivelled-up old virgin.'

'Sylvia!' exclaimed her husband. 'Was that really necessary?'

'Sorry, Silas, but she gets right up my nose. Anyhow,

54

she stopped attending every meeting after a bit. There was nothing exciting enough for her to join in with regularly, and she only shows up now when the activity or subject under discussion is of particular interest to her.'

'Can you tell me about anyone else who might have been there that night?'

Carmichael's cup finally overbalanced, and a few minutes were spent mopping up the dregs of tea and getting him a side table while his cup was refilled, and the sugar was passed to him again, only reluctantly this time. After he'd sweetened his second cup, the bowl was nearly empty. 'I'm so sorry, Sylvia,' Carmichael apologised. 'It was what you said about that Sutherland woman that made me laugh, and off it went, like a toboggan down a hill.'

'Never you mind, Sergeant. Now, where were we? Ah, yes, who might have been in the church on Friday? Well, Yvonne Pooley, without doubt. She's choir mistress and organist; oh, and if she couldn't play, it would be Willard Scardifield, although he and his wife, Thea, would both have been there anyway, as they both sing in the choir.

'Elodie Sutherland is in it, and Ian Brown, the crucifer, he sits in on tenor, as Albert is … was a bass. Polly Garfield and her eight-year-old daughter, who's a Brownie, come quite often, and there are some other slightly older children who attend – which of course you know, because of Chelsea Winter.'

'We didn't know about other teenagers and older children. Do you think you could give their names and addresses to Sergeant Carmichael?'

'I'll do my best, but you'd do better to call on Mrs Pooley. She has a register with everyone's names and addresses, even those who only come occasionally.'

'Thank you very much, Sylvia,' said Falconer, when Carmichael had finally finished scribbling in his notebook, and had mugged their hostess for a third cup of tea, which did, in fact, empty her sugar bowl, much to his and her embarrassment – his, because he had used it all, and hers, because she had not envisaged getting such a sweet-toothed visitor this afternoon. She would have to remember his habit of having six spoonfuls, should they return to question them again.

Silas saw them out of the door and down the garden path, where they turned their steps towards the Old Bakery down Dryden's Passage to speak to Polly Garfield. They had decided to walk to all the houses on their list as Ford Hollow was such a tiny village. It was a nice day with no sign yet of autumn, and they wanted to enjoy the sunshine while they still could. It was a long time to next spring, so any late good weather was to be cherished when it occurred.

Polly answered the door with her usual broad smile. She was someone whose glass was always half, if not three-quarters, full. When she saw their warrant cards, she said in a cheerful and inviting voice, 'Come on in. I'll put the kettle on, and there're some jam tarts just finishing off in the oven. If you want to wait for them to cool a bit, you can have some.'

Falconer tried to wave away the idea of another drink but, having seen the pleading look on Carmichael's face, he relented, and they chose coffee this time. Polly soon came through with a tray and the news that she had just left the jam tarts out to cool.

Mrs Garfield was in her mid-forties and married, very happily, for the second time. She had a daughter from her first marriage who was grown-up and had moved away from home, and an eight-year-old from her second. Her house smelled fresh and was spotlessly clean. Her husband was manager of a local nursery.

'You were lucky to catch me,' she told them. 'I'm a cleaner, and I've got all sorts of odd hours. In fact, if it wasn't for the reason you're here, I wouldn't be either.' She looked at their puzzled faces and explained, 'On

Saturday, I usually do a bit of shopping for Mr Burton, then give him a lick and a polish inside the house. It seems strange not to be doing that today. He seemed perfectly all right at choir practice last night.'

'I'm afraid it wasn't an accident or natural causes, Polly, if you don't mind me calling you that. I'm afraid the old chap was murdered.'

'Oh my God!' squeaked the woman. 'Who, in the name of all that's holy, would kill a harmless old man like that? Surely no one from round here?'

'That's what we're trying to find out. Now, did you go to choir practice last night? From what you've said, I assume you did.'

'I did, indeed, but my daughter stayed at home because she had a bit of a cough, and I didn't want her annoying Mrs Pooley. She's ever so easy to get going, you know.'

'Can you tell me who else was there?' asked Falconer, wondering how many other times he was going to have to ask his question. He was glad it wasn't a choral society, or it would take days.

When they had learnt everything they could from her, they stood to leave, and were invited to help themselves on the way out to a jam tart or two.

Back in the car, Falconer said, 'You were lucky she had some antiseptic cream for those burns, and a couple of plasters. You should know by your age that hot jam sticks like muck to a blanket, and it burns like hell.'

'I know it now, sir,' replied Carmichael, somewhat indistinctly, as he had burnt his tongue, and was sucking a finger which was only slightly singed.

'How you managed to eat three while she was getting out the first aid kit, I shall never understand. You must have an asbestos gullet.'

Rev. Florrie didn't manage to get out on time but, then, it didn't matter, as the person she had being going to visit turned up on her doorstep, a hungry look on her face. Opening the door, she said, 'Hello, Miss Sutherland. Do come in. What can I do for you? I was coming to see you anyway.'

'I know, but I'd rather get it sorted sooner than later, and in private,' she replied, looking around furtively to see if there was anyone listening from the staircase or the sitting room.

'What is it? Is it important?'

'Yes, very. You see, Albert Burton was head chorister because of his age. That position should be mine now, as I'm next in age – not that I'm terribly old, just that so many of the members are so young. Will you appoint me to the position, please, Vicar?'

'I don't see why you shouldn't take over. Does it have to be ratified by the PCC or the choir mistress?' asked Florrie, quite taken aback by the other woman's rather cold-hearted determination, and not sure yet how things were run in this parish.

'It's up to you, because it's usually done on seniority, and that means me.' The woman looked almost demented with anxiety.

'OK, Miss Sutherland, I hereby appoint you as chief chorister.' Elodie Sutherland grabbed Florrie's hand and began pumping it up and down. 'You won't regret this, Vicar. I shan't let you down. I'll be the best head chorister the church has ever had.'

When she finally left, Florrie leant up against the hall wall, almost exhausted by the woman's depth of emotion. Still, at least she could cross her off the visiting list, as her mother had given up home communion. What an empty and sterile life she must lead, though, if this appointment meant so much to her.

She'd hardly caught her breath when there was another person knocking and ringing at the door. How impatient so many of these people seemed, to get her attention. Maybe it was symptomatic of not having had a parish priest for some time. Maybe that would even go in her favour with them accepting a female vicar?

When she answered what sounded like an urgent summons, she found Rev. Monaghan on the doorstep. She had only met him briefly a couple of times before her appointment to the parish, and she observed him closely now. His cassock had a few food stains on it, his hair badly needed a cut, and his beard looked filthy, with bits of food – she presumed it was food – making a nest in its tangled bush. 'Come in,' she invited him, then reeled back as he passed her in the doorway. The man had a chronic BO problem, emphasised even more by the large round damp marks under his arms.

He breezed aromatically past her and headed for the living room. 'In here, if you don't mind,' she instructed, directing him to the kitchen. 'I spend a lot of time in here and, as I'm probably about to make tea for you, we might as well sit out here.'

With a grunt of approval, he followed her and took a chair at the wooden table. 'You've certainly had a baptism of fire,' he commented, grinning inanely at her. 'Must seem like old times to you, after your last parish,' he added, somewhat undiplomatically.

'I'd rather not discuss that, if you don't mind,' Florrie replied, looking down at her ankles as Kelly Finn began to weave her elegant body between them. What bad form that comment was. 'Do you take sugar?'

'What else could keep me so sweet?' he answered, with a rather unpleasant leer. Kelly Finn made her way across to this stranger, hissed, and shot out of the room as if her tail were on fire. 'Highly strung?' he asked, looking after the retreating ball of fur.

'Not usually,' said Florrie, already beginning to feel uneasy in the man's company. 'Here's the tea. What can I do for you?' she asked, sitting down.

'Oh, I'm sure there's an awful lot you could do for me,' he said, and she felt a hand on her knee.

'I'd rather you didn't do that,' she said, in a voice made shrill with shock.

'There's no need to be shy,' he leered across the table at her, and his hand began to caress her knee.' Oh my God, she thought. He's got the worst case of bad breath I've ever come across. I've got to do something drastic to put an end to this.

Kicking out for all she was worth, and managing to get him right on the fork on his trousers, she rose almost as quickly as he did. 'I think you'd better go, and we'll meet on more neutral ground, if you don't mind.'

'I haven't really time to stay for tea,' he replied, his body slightly bent with the pain she had inflicted. 'I just wanted to welcome you to your new parish.' In fact, if he were alone, she was sure he would have been caressing his crown jewels after the assault they had just suffered. Well, it served him right. How dare he assume she would be a sucker for his very limited charms. And he had no intention of welcoming her to the parish! He just wanted to introduce himself to her body.

'I'm sure you can see yourself out. I need to get ready for some parish visiting.'

When he had gone, she gently coaxed her beloved cat out from under the stairs, where she had retreated to hide from this hideously fragrant monster. 'It's all right, my darling, the nasty man's gone now, and it's safe to come to Mummy.' She'd have to ask around about this predatory cleric.

Wheel Cottage, although having its postal address in the High Street, it was actually on the corner of this and Dryden's Passage, so the two detectives had, of necessity, walked past the choir mistress' house to reach Polly Garfield's. Fortunately, she was at home and, as was only hospitable, offered them some refreshment.

Falconer was quick with his polite refusal. 'No, thank you very much, Mrs Pooley. We're awash from the other interviews we've conducted this morning and, if we had just another half a cup, I think we'd both overflow.'

'Your sergeant seems to have hurt himself. Is he all right?'

'He's fine, thank you for asking. He just got himself into a bit of a jam,' replied the inspector, smiling knowingly. 'Now, we'd like you to tell us the names and address of all the people who attended choir practice on Friday evening. You know why we're here?'

'I do. So tragic, although he was an old fussbudget, always trying to tell me how a thing should be sung. I certainly shan't miss that, although the choir will miss his voice.'

'He was a nuisance?' asked Carmichael, suddenly showing an interest now he had a few moments when he wasn't writing down names and addresses.

'Not really. It was just that he'd sung for so many decades, that he had his own ideas from previous choirs, about how things should be done. He wasn't what you'd really call a nuisance; rather like a quiet voice that did its best to undermine me on some occasions.'

At this point, this not being a school day, two children aged about five and eight rushed into the room, stared at the two policemen, and began to giggle helplessly. 'Jeffrey, Michelle, go outside again and play. It's very rude to interrupt when I've got visitors.'

'We thought it might have been that vicar man with the beard who so upset you at Christmas, and made you very cross for ages,' offered the older child, the girl, and Falconer looked at Mrs Pooley pointedly as she blushed a gentle pink.

'Rev. Monaghan,' she explained. 'He's head of the team ministry for not just Ford Hollow, but Carsfold, where he lives, Downland Haven, and Coldwater Pryors.'

'And he's a bit of a handful, is he?'

'It's a bit of handful that he's after,' replied Mrs Pooley, her colour deepening at the memory. 'No woman under ninety is safe from him and his wandering hands. He's an absolute menace, but the bishop thinks he's the bee's knees in increasing ailing congregations, and won't hear a word against him. I think, now we've got a woman vicar, I might have a word with her about him, and see if she can't get the women of all the parishes to get up a petition.'

Young Jeffrey re-entered the room at that moment, looking thoughtful. 'What is it, dear?' she asked.

'They've not come about the new houses that you don't want anyone to build, have they?' he enquired, with a young child's innocence.

'No, dear. Now go and play with your sister until Mummy's finished.'

'What houses?' asked Falconer, his interest piqued.

'I'm afraid that takes up much of my free time at the moment. There's an old farm at the end of Pig Lane where the land became useless for animals or growing because of the flooding from the Little Darle. Eventually the farmer gave up and moved out – retired.

'Somehow, he's been able to get someone to take the land off his hands – some company called Landbank Ltd – and they've sold it off in little parcels to greedy people hoping to make a fortune when they get a change of use to development land instead of agricultural.'

'Well, that shouldn't be easy, should it?' asked the inspector. 'An estate of new houses here would be disastrous. I mean, where's the infrastructure to support it? What about the ford? What about the Little Darle?' He'd heard about the scheme from Florrie but he wanted to hear it in the woman's own words.

'Nothing's impossible when you've got friends in high

places, and can prove that the land is no longer fit for agricultural use. The Little Darle will probably be diverted, and the ford will dry up, only to flood in any heavy winter rain, it's so low-lying. There are bound to be backhanders involved. I'm trying to drum as much interest as I can for an official protest, but it's very time-consuming.'

'Have you got the PCC involved?' He was definitely interested now. He didn't like little people being bulldozed just because they didn't have big bucks.

'Not as yet,' she replied, her eyes lighting up.

'What about the parish council?'

'I could do, couldn't I?'

'Have you spoken to your local MP?'

'Crooked as a corkscrew. I'm sure he's at the bottom of this.'

'What about the district or county councils?'

'Not so sure about them. There's bound to be a mole in the planning committee, but you never know who you can and who you can't trust.'

'Give it a go,' Falconer urged her. 'If you leak a fictitious piece of information to one person at a time, you'll soon find out who's not on your side.'

'You are sneaky, aren't you? Thanks. I'll do that,' replied Mrs Pooley, and she actually smiled at them.

'Thanks for your list of choir members. If you can think of anything or remember anything, here's my card,' said Falconer, handing her one. 'By the way, why did you have to leave church early on Friday – I believe you mentioned that you did.'

'I was expecting an important phone call.'

'From whom?'

'From my mother. She was getting the results of her final test for breast cancer yesterday. She's been having treatment on and off for years.'

'And how is she?'

'She's been cleared, which is great. What isn't so good, is that she never rang me until a quarter to eleven, having gone out to celebrate with some friends. Since I've heard about Albert's death, I've worried myself sick about whether he'd still be alive if I'd stayed behind, as usual, to lock up.'

'So, who was going to lock up?'

'Me! Later on! I was in such a fury with my mother, though, that I completely forgot, then I heard the next morning about poor old Mr Burton, and realised it simply didn't matter any more. Events had overtaken me.'

'Please don't let it worry you too much. Whoever did this would no doubt have got inside the church and done exactly what was done before you got back,' Falconer soothed her with utter sincerity.

'Do you really think so?' she asked.

'I do.'

'And so do I,' chimed in Carmichael.

'Thank you so much, and if I think of anything else, I'll get in touch.'

'Thank you again for your time.'

Chapter Six

Saturday Afternoon

Having got into the High Street proper, the two representatives of law and order espied The Plume of Feathers, and immediately changed their hastily made plans to go back to Castle Farthing for lunch. It would save a lot of time, and they would easily finish this first round of questioning today if they ate lunch there. They'd even be able to speak to the landlord and his wife and kill two birds with one stone while they ate.

Both were in evidence behind the bar, the pub with a fair number of customers for a Saturday lunchtime, most of them, no doubt, to see what gossip they could pick up about the local murder. Spotting immediately who their most recent arrivals were, the couple behind the bar introduced themselves as Gail and Clive Davies.

Taking their orders for a ploughman's lunch and an orange squash apiece, she disappeared into the back of the pub. This was one perfect part of Falconer and Carmichael's partnership – neither of them was very fond of alcohol, and as they felt the same way, they could be honest about it when they were out and about.

Taking stools at the bar when they were served, Falconer asked them what they knew about the events of the previous Friday evening.

'Nothing much,' replied Gail, 'except the phone call to let us know that Chelsea would be staying with the vicar for the night. Anyone in the village would have done the same. They all know where to find Joel and Lisa on a Friday evening – or a Saturday, or a Sunday – in fact, most evenings they're in here. I feel sorry for that kid sometimes. It can't be a lot of fun with a mum and a stepdad who are both alcoholics. How she ever gets fed or gets her clothes washed I've no idea.'

'Do the parents work?'

'You must be kidding! Not when there are benefits available, and plenty of work on the black. At least with a life like that you can choose your own hours, and don't have to get up with a hangover to be anywhere else early.'

'They work on the black, do they?'

'It's only what I've heard,' replied Gail, suddenly becoming cagey as she realised she was talking about two of her best customers to somebody official. 'I think Joel does a bit of lawn-mowing in summer, and some odd jobs for people who can't do them themselves – nothing serious.'

'And Lisa?' The inspector was determined to get as much information as he could before his source dried up completely.

'A bit of cleaning here and there, but nothing regular. Yes, Ted, what can I get you?' She moved off down the bar with the last of this statement, and Falconer asked Carmichael if he knew where Clive was.

'V las tm I soim …'

'OK, finish your mouthful first, or I'll never understand a word you say.'

Swallowing hard, the sergeant said, 'The last time I saw him he was going outside for a smoke.'

'How did you know it was for a cigarette?'

'Because of the number of customers who saw him, and made mimes of drawing on one, then blowing out invisible smoke.'

'Fair dos. Ah, here he comes now. Mr Davies! Clive!' Falconer called out to the landlord, raising an arm and waving; very uncharacteristic behaviour, but it brought results.

'What can I do for you gentlemen?' asked Clive, slipping back behind the bar.

'Same again for me,' said Carmichael, firmly.

'Another orange squash?'

'And another ploughman's, if you don't mind.'

'By George, you're hungry,' commented Davies, only for Falconer to reply, 'He always is. Eats like a horse but never puts on an ounce.'

'He's a big lad,' was Davies' come-back, 'and there's plenty of food in the kitchen. Gail, same again for the sergeant – including the food. Now, what can I do for you?'

'We're just here to confirm anything you know about what happened on Friday night.'

'Only that there was a call for us to tell the Jells that their daughter would be staying over at the vicarage. Anyone here would have known where to call. There was no way they would've been at home on a Friday night.'

'That's what your wife said.'

'Small village. We all know each other's habits.'

'So there's nothing else you can tell us?'

'Only that Joel and Lisa didn't give a flying doo-dah where Chelsea spent the night, provided she didn't get in the way of them and their beloved booze. Poor kid. She must have a helluva life with those two.'

'That's definitely the impression we're getting. We'll pop along for a word when we've finished here, see if we can't put the fear of God into them about neglect.'

'Oh, the old cow's got you there. Chelsea's just turned sixteen. She reckons she's untouchable,' replied Lisa, who had just sidled up beside her husband to make sure she didn't miss anything.

'There're all sorts of things I could threaten her with that she's not even heard of,' replied Falconer, his face a mask of disapproval. 'Come on, Carmichael, get that last pickled onion down your neck and let's get on our way. People to interview, crimes to solve. Come along, Gannet.'

'Yes, sir,' agreed the sergeant chewing furiously on his pickle and having his eyes water in response to such a large mouthful of the spicy vegetable.

The turning down Drovers Way was the first on the right from the pub, off the Fallow Fold Road, and Bluebell Cottage was the first tiny cottage after Albert's former home. Carmichael knocked on the door, wondering how a sixteen-year-old could exist in such a minute dwelling with two alcoholic adults. There was just nowhere in this village for kids to go to get away from their parents.

It was Chelsea who opened the door, recognising them from the night before, and saying she'd have to get her mum and Joel up, as they were still in bed. 'At this time?' queried the inspector. 'We've already had our lunch.'

'It's the same every weekend,' she confirmed with a heavy sigh. 'Sit down and I'll take a couple of coffees up and some paracetamol, and see if I can get them back into the land of the living.' There had been no living room to direct them to, as the front doors opened directly into the only room downstairs apart from the kitchen.

Chelsea shortly mounted the stairs, which went up between the two rooms, and they could hear sounds of movement upstairs, then raised voices. She was soon down again, her face slightly flushed. 'They'll be down in a moment,' she said. 'Can I get you anything?'

'We've just had lunch at The Plume of Feathers, but thank you anyway, Chelsea,' ventured Carmichael, smiling at her in a friendly fashion. He felt so sorry for her when he thought of his own happy household, and wondered how she managed to carry on living like this.

Upstairs there was some language that was probably better being muffled by the intervening floorboards, then a heavy clumping down the stairs. Eventually, two dishevelled figures appeared in the room wearing unsavoury dressing gowns and slippers, their hair seriously disarranged and sticking up every which way, which wasn't surprising considering that the two policemen had had to help Mrs Jell upstairs to bed the night before. Falconer recalled the incident with a little sneer of distaste.

'What the hell do you two want?' asked Joel aggressively.

'You know we were in the pub until nearly closing time last night, so what do you expect to get from us? We were in no state to commit murder,' claimed his wife.

'Do you remember coming home?'

'Not exactly, but we must've done, or we wouldn't be here,' she said sarcastically.

'There's been many a crime – even murder – committed while under the influence of alcohol, with no memory whatsoever the next day,' stated Falconer in his most authoritative voice. 'How can you be a hundred per cent sure that you didn't just twist the old man's neck just to see how far round it would go?'

Carmichael looked at the inspector with surprise. This wasn't like him at all. 'And what's more,' he continued, the sergeant too surprised to butt in, 'Chelsea may be sixteen, but I'll do everything in my power involving social services to see that she is treated a bit better than she is at present. I shall get them to call round regularly, and I shall call round myself, as will my sergeant. If I don't see some improvement in her existence, I'll have a place found for her in a juvenile hostel, so that at least she won't have to witness your disgusting drunken behaviour on a regular basis.'

'You can't do that!' yelled Joel.

'*You're* not even her father,' stated Falconer.

'Well, I'm her mother, and you can't take her away from me,' chimed in Lisa.

'I think you'd be surprised what we can do, if we rattle

enough cages and cause a sufficient stink. We could make all kinds of changes.' Carmichael's mouth was literally hanging open at this completely unveiled threat.

'I'll certainly get one of the volunteers from Alcoholics Anonymous to pay you a visit,' Falconer concluded, 'because you obviously need help.'

That left both the Jells speechless. Chelsea was the first one to speak after the inspector's little outburst. 'I'm all right, really. If things get any worse, I've got a promise from a friend's mum that I can go and stay there.'

'Chelsea!' called her mother, and promptly burst into tears.

'You've got to change – both of you – or I won't be living here much longer. I can't take any more.'

Lisa Jell held out her arms, and Chelsea walked over to her. At this signal, the two detectives left, closing the door behind them. 'You don't really believe that, sir, do you?' asked Carmichael, 'About people doing things when they're drunk and not remembering – even murder.'

'It's the absolute truth. There are plenty of cases all over the world where people have committed murder while drunk or under the influence of drugs, that they have no recall at all about the next day.'

'I don't give a stuff, and if you want to do something about our Chelsea, try to get her away from that bloody bunch of God-botherers at the church. They're putting a load of weird ideas into her head that are absolutely ridiculous,' called the voice of Lisa Jell through a window she had just opened.

'Like what?' Here, Falconer was curious.

'She went banging on at me and Joel for the best part of a year that she wanted to learn to play the damned organ. Have you ever heard of anything so ridiculous? Anyway, I gave in, in the end, and went to see that stuck-up cow Yvonne Pooley. Not only did she want to charge a ridiculously high price, but she said she didn't have time at the moment, and that she'd need to be paid a term in advance. A term!

'And there'd be no refunds if Chelsea was sick or missed a lesson for any reason. Have you ever heard of anything so greedy? Well, that was it. I'd done my bit in going round there and crawling to Mrs High-and-Mighty choir mistress. I wasn't going to have anything more to do with it.'

'I asked if you'd say something to Mr Scardifield,' Chelsea suddenly piped up. 'He's the assistant organist, so he might have done it.'

'Yeah, and pigs might fly to the moon. You ask him, if you're so desperate to get even more involved with that holier-than-thou bunch of hypocrites.'

After this exchange, Chelsea burst into tears and took herself off upstairs, presumably to her room.

Carmichael swallowed hard, then asked, with remarkable simplicity after what they had just witnessed, 'Who's next, sir?'

Chapter Seven

Still Saturday afternoon

'We've got three more to do,' Falconer informed Carmichael. 'The Scardifields, Ian Brown, and both the Sutherlands. We'll take the Scardifields first. Turn left at the end of this road, back to the High Street, then left, and we should find Clouds on our left.'

They did, and it was Willard who opened the door to them. After brief introductions, he invited them in and introduced them to his wife, Thea, a tiny woman who was dwarfed by her husband's stature. He was a good six feet two inches tall, she little more than five feet, and slightly built as well. Both had grey hair and were obviously retired.

Once seated in two very comfortable wing chairs, they were brought tea by Thea while Willard explained their relationship with the church. 'We're both in the choir. Thea is in the MU as well, and I'm on the PCC. I'm also assistant organist – when I'm allowed to play it. That Mrs Pooley is fiercely jealous of her position, you know. Ah, thanks, how lovely,' he finished, as his wife re-entered the room laden down with a tray with all the accoutrements of tea, including a fortunately full sugar bowl.

'I was just telling the inspector and sergeant about our relationship with the church.' His wife's unexpected reply was, 'Pah!'

'I beg your pardon?' he asked his wife.

'It's that blasted Mothers' Union,' she replied. 'It was

stretching it a bit when we let Sylvia Slater come to meetings, but now – and I've no idea how, as I'm supposed to be its nominal head – that awful Sutherland woman's been coming along, and she's never had anything to do with children. At least Sylvia has a whole pack of nieces and nephews who are now producing children of their own. The Sutherland woman would faint if anyone asked her to change a nappy or bath a baby. She's not even married, let alone a mother, and I don't believe she has any brothers or sisters either, so she can't even be an auntie.'

'Good heavens, woman! Where's that all come from? Why didn't you say something to me sooner?'

'There was no point, but now we've got a new vicar and she's a woman, so I think I'll go and see her sometime, to see how she feels about non-mothers attending MU meetings.'

'Good heavens, is it really that important?'

'To me it is, Willard. To me it is.'

'Mr and Mrs Scardifield,' said Falconer after clearing his throat loudly while Carmichael slurped tea noisily in the other chair. 'We've come here to ask you if you have any idea what may have happened on Friday night, what time you left the church, who was still there, and if you saw anyone hanging about outside.'

'Sorry, Inspector. As far as I remember, we left about eight thirty. The practice was longer than usual because we were looking at a new piece …' offered Willard.

'And not every chorister can read music,' broke in Thea, somewhat angrily. 'I just don't understand why that Pooley woman doesn't give them lessons in music-reading. It would make things so much easier, instead of them having to learn everything new by heart. What will happen when the younger girls' voices go down and they can't reach soprano range any more, I have no idea. That Sutherland woman should really be a first alto, but she won't, even though she reads reasonably well.'

74

'Thea, our visitors are policemen, not agony aunts. Do you think you could keep your grievances to yourself and concentrate on what we've been asked?' said Willard pointedly. 'I've said we left about half past eight.'

Thea seemed to gather herself together, then agreed with him.

'And who was still in the church?' Falconer reiterated, in case they had lost track of the information he had requested.

'The children had all been taken home by parents, who had been waiting for quite a long time. Mrs Pooley had to go, as she said she was expecting a phone call, I think she said. Albert was obviously there, and I think there were a few others, but I can't recall who.'

Thea took up the tale. 'I'd put a casserole in the oven for us for after the practice, and we shot off rather, because I was beginning to suspect that it would have dried out what with the practice going so over time.'

'And had it?' asked Carmichael, always interested in anything to do with food.

'No, it was perfectly all right. I'd been sensible enough to leave it in at a very low heat, and the meat was exceptionally tender,' Thea informed the sergeant with a smile.

'Excuse me, but does that mean that you don't remember who was left behind when you went home?' asked Falconer, feeling quite irritated about the way they kept wandering away from the subject.

'That's right, Inspector,' confirmed Willard.

'And did you notice anyone hanging around outside, or who might be on their way to the church?'

'I didn't, Inspector,' replied Thea. 'Did you, dear?'

Willard furrowed his brows, then said, 'No. No one. If we hadn't needed to rush off, I'd have taken the opportunity for a quick play at the organ. I very rarely get the opportunity, as Mrs Pooley guards it so jealously, and is mysteriously unavailable with the church key when I've got time on my hands.'

'Do you know if Mr Burton had any enemies, or if anyone had a particular grudge against him?' Falconer wasn't giving up that easily.

'He was too old to have enemies,' replied Willard a tad pompously. 'And I should think that just about everyone had some sort of a grudge against him. At his age, he must have fallen out, at some time or another, with just about every other resident of Ford Hollow.'

So that was that. 'If either of you think of something that may be pertinent to our enquiries, or remember something from Friday evening, please contact us at the police station in Market Darley. Here's my card,' said Falconer in a defeated voice. They had got nowhere again. Maybe they'd strike lucky elsewhere.

'Oh, by the way, we'll not be around after next Saturday, as we're visiting our daughter in France on a short late break, in case you need to speak to us again. We'll only be gone a few days, though.'

Ian Brown, who was their next interviewee, had his house just the other side of the right-hand turn of Dairy House Road. 'There we go, Carmichael. Mon Repos. Let's see how rested he is this sunny Saturday.' His mood had cleared instantly at the thought of someone else to interview. He was even switched on enough not to pronounce the s at the end of the house name, which puzzled Carmichael.

'You only pronounce a consonant at the end of a French word if it's followed by a vowel, and then only sometimes. It's a bit of a minefield, but "Mon Repos" hasn't anything after it, so you don't pronounce the s – Mon Rep*oh*.'

'I'm glad I didn't do French at school,' the sergeant replied. 'We were taught that if a letter's there, then you pronounce it.' Falconer had his mouth half-open, then decided to shut it again. This was not the time or the place to start a discussion on pronunciation that could go on for days with Carmichael, and might have repercussions for months after.

They found Ian Brown mowing his front lawn. 'Just giving it a quick cut in case the weather turns and I don't get the chance again until spring,' he explained, as he led them into the house. 'Heard what happened to old Mr Burton. Shocking, isn't it, and in a little place like this. It's almost unbelievable.'

'I thought you sang with the choir, Mr Brown,' said Falconer. Carmichael said nothing. He was too busy sharpening his pencil into his pocket. Kerry would have a fit, but not many people smoked any more so he could hardly ask for an ashtray.

'I do, but I couldn't make last night's practice, much to my chagrin,' he replied.

'Something more important came up?'

'You could say that. I had one of my heads.' Looking at their puzzled faces, he went on, 'I suffer, occasionally, from migraine. If I don't do something about it immediately, my vision goes and I start vomiting like a fountain, so I took a couple of my tablets, drew the bedroom curtains, and spent the evening lying on the bed. Fortunately they don't last for days, like some people's do, and a good night's sleep normally sees them off.'

'Do you get them often?'

'Only once every couple of months or so, but if I don't take something immediately, I get big spiky patterns across the vision in my left eye, and the only thing I can do then is fetch a bucket and lock myself away.'

'Very bad luck, sir. We wondered what you could tell us about Mr Burton. Did you know him well, singing in the choir with him?'

'Not really. He was bass and I'm a tenor, so we sat a little apart to spread the male sound, with Willard

Scardifield between us. He could manage tenor or bass, so he just chose which part he liked the best and sung that.'

'And being crucifer didn't interfere with you singing with the choir?'

'Not really. We all processed up the aisle singing at the beginning of service, and we all processed down the aisle singing at the end of the service, unless there was processional organ music. It was just that I couldn't hold a hymn book and carry the cross, so if it was something I didn't know very well, I'd either have to learn it *tout de suite*, or mime.'

'Do you know if anyone had had a fall out with Mr Burton recently?'

'It was impossible to fall out with him in recent years. If you tried to, he'd just shut up, smile, and walk away. He'd had enough of the bad in his life not to want any more. Did you know his mother died when he was away fighting in the war, and his father just after Albert married? His wife died when their son was twelve, and he had to bring him up single-handed. Then, when he was grown up, his son moved away to London, and he only sees his father about twice a year, to my knowledge.'

'And the son never married?'

'Nope. So there was no daughter-in-law to fuss around, and no grandchildren for Albert.'

Carmichael was terribly moved by this tale of loss and loneliness, and nearly lost his place in his notes. 'He's been dogged by bad luck all his life, really, then?' asked Falconer, discreetly kicking Carmichael on the ankle to regain his concentration on the job at hand.

'Mr Burton wouldn't have said so. He said he was lucky to have met and married such a wonderful woman, and privileged to have brought up her son. He was also so passionate about his church music, sometimes, he lived in another world: a world full of heavenly harmonies and divine melodies. I think, on the whole, he was happy with his lot, although a lot of people would have complained and moaned like hell.'

'What a brave man,' murmured Carmichael.

'Albert was a pragmatist, and just got on with what life threw at him, and made the best of what he'd got. He was so chuffed about those new hymn books of his, that he put them in the saddlebag of his bicycle and brought them to church a month or so ago, so that the whole choir could have a look at them. He told Mrs Pooley if she ever wanted to use anything out of them, he'd lend them to her so they could be copied for us lot.'

'That was very generous of him,' said Falconer.

'So it was, and she threw that back in his face, the miserable old bitch. She told him it was illegal to use copied music in a live performance, and that she'd do no such thing.'

'How did he take that?'

'He just shrugged and said the offer was open if she wanted to take him up on it. He wasn't one to take offence, although I would have, if it had happened to me.'

'Thank you very much, Mr Brown. What you've told us has been very helpful. If you should think of anything else, please don't hesitate to call. Here's my card.'

'Poor old man,' said Carmichael, *sotto voce*, as they were leaving.

'Life did seem to have it in for him, didn't it? And now for the Sutherland ladies. I wonder what we shall find out there? Look, just along here. The house is called Lizanben. Yuck!'

'Double yuck!' agreed Carmichael.

The daughter of the household answered their summons at the door with an expression that could only be described as beatific. 'Do come in, gentlemen,' she bade them, after they had produced their warrant cards. 'It's so important to check identification these days, especially being two vulnerable ladies living alone, with no man to protect them,' she said, in a superior voice, still with that saintly, other-worldly expression on her face.

Inside, the house was a perfect museum of sixties modernism, perfectly preserved, if a little ragged round the edges here and there. In an armchair shaped like a pair of lips sat a very old woman wrinkled like an ancient apple, her hair perfectly white. 'This is my mother,' introduced Elodie Sutherland. 'She used to be cutting-edge in her ideas of interior décor,' she said, whether as explanation or apology, neither Falconer nor Carmichael was sure.

'How lovely,' croaked the old crone. 'Two young men come to visit us. Aren't we lucky girls, Elodie?'

'They're policemen, Mummy, come about what I told you happened to Albert.'

'Shame,' sighed the old woman, shaking her head. 'I remember him when he was a young man, just come back from the war, when he first moved here. He was quite handsome.'

'Do you?' asked Falconer. 'What was he like?'

'Always cheerful, that's what I remember; always had a smile on his face, and he loved his music, even back then,' she replied with a faraway look in her eyes.

'When did you last see him?'

'About ten years ago,' she replied, without a trace of irony in her voice. 'I don't get out and about like I used to, and neither did Albert, I guess.'

That scuppered that line of enquiry. 'What about you, Miss Sutherland? You were at choir practice on Friday, weren't you?' He wasn't giving up that easily. His best chance still lay ahead of him.

'I was, of course, there. They need me, you know, as someone who reads music well. I see myself as a sort of guide for the younger ones.' She was really putting it on. 'Did you know that I've been appointed new head chorister? Of course I'm very honoured, and I shall take

80

my role very seriously, maybe setting up some music-reading classes for the younger ones. I know poor, overworked Mrs Pooley doesn't have the time. I'm also a lay reader, you know?'

'That's very generous of you, Miss Sutherland. Now, can you tell me when you left the church that evening?'

'I'm not sure. It ended a bit later than normal, and I never wear a watch in church – it seems, somehow, sacrilegious, to keep an eye on the time when one is in God's house.'

Oh, heaven help us, thought Falconer. She really is holier than thou. I hope we can get some straight answers from her and get out of here, or she'll drive me to commit the very ungentlemanly act of slapping her round the face and telling her to get a grip.

'Oh, I know it's an appointment in seniority mainly, but even without that, I'd have been the obvious choice, once Albert was no longer with us. Such a tragedy.' At this, she removed a handkerchief from her cardigan pocket and pretended to wipe away her crocodile tears.

'Where was Mr Burton when you left?' Let's get real here, thought Falconer, and not get bogged down in false mourning.

'I can't recall, you know. I was more worried about Mummy being left alone longer than normal,' she replied, with perfect logic.

'I was worried about her, too. She could've been raped on her way home,' chimed in Mummy.

'So, you're not sure when you left, and you don't remember where Mr Burton was when you did?' Falconer asked her, just for clarification.

'That's right. But, then, I didn't know it was going to be important, did I? How was I to know the old man was going to be murdered? Will there be anything else, as neither of us can be of any further help to you?'

'No. We'll leave you in peace now,' replied Falconer,

somewhat relieved that they hadn't got stuck there listening to a lecture about how pious the younger Sutherland woman was. Although he had feared they would get stuck there, they had finished a little earlier than he had anticipated, and Carmichael, taking advantage of this, asked him round to his place for a glass of squash to wash away the taste of all that tea.

'Well, I suppose we didn't call in at lunchtime and I haven't seen Kerry for a while. Yes, that would be very nice. And talking about all that tea, not to mention the coffee, how many spoonfuls of sugar do you reckon you've got through today?'

'Somewhere between fifty and infinity,' answered Carmichael, with an impish grin.

'Why you don't weight twenty stone and waddle, I shall never understand. I know you're a big lad,' – at six feet five and a half, he certainly was – 'but if my car gobbled fuel the way your body seems to need to, I'd never be able to afford to drive anywhere further than the boundary of my garden.'

'I just can't help it, sir. I feel really sorry for people who have to go on a diet.'

And I bet they really love you, thought the inspector, a little sourly, as he had to watch his weight diligently so that he didn't pile on the pounds. He never used kilos, because it made everything sound lighter than it did in pounds, and he knew that that was the slippery slope to hell.

As Falconer stepped into Jasmine Cottage, Carmichael's home in Castle Farthing, instead of greeting Kerry and the children as he had planned to , being an honorary uncle and actual godfather, he shouted quite loudly, making the youngest, Harriet, who wasn't yet a year old, jump, and burst into tears.

'What the hell is that animated cocktail sausage doing

in your house, Carmichael. I thought it had gone to the RSPCA for rehoming.' The Dachshund in question had belonged to someone involved in their last case, and Falconer had thought never to set eyes on it again.

'They did rehome him, sir – to me.' Carmichael paused, then explained, almost as way of apology, 'I couldn't leave Dipsy Daxie to go to just any old home, so I went and rescued him and brought him here. We got on together very well whenever we met before, and I thought he'd like it here.'

'With your three children, two other dogs, and a wife expecting twins? Ah, Kerry, good evening. How are you keeping? My, you're looking bonny,' he changed the subject, as Carmichael's other half appeared from the kitchen, already looking as round as an apple, although the babies were not due until early the following year. 'Is she supposed to be that big at this stage?' the inspector whispered to his sergeant while Kerry tended to her upset daughter.

'It's normal if you've already been stretched several times, and are sprouting two this time,' replied Carmichael, also *sotto voce*.

'There, there,' Kerry soothed Harriet. 'Look, it's only your Uncle Harry come to visit.' At this, she held Harriet out for Falconer to take from her, whereupon the little one cried even harder, and squirmed in her mother's arms.

'It is a long time since she's seen me,' said Falconer by way of excuse. 'Maybe if I visited more regularly, she'd get to know me better.' No way was he going to invite the entire Carmichael clan to visit his immaculate dwelling. He was by now sat on the sofa, with a boy at each side of him, as Kerry's sons from her first marriage, whom Carmichael had formally adopted, had become quite fond of him.

'We've just popped in to say hello, and to see if we can have a long cool drink,' Carmichael explained, in case she was wondering why the two of them had come back to the house.

'You take Harriet and I'll get you both something. It's been very warm for the time of year today, hasn't it?' she called over her shoulder as she went back into the kitchen. She came back a minute or so later with two long glasses filled with apple juice and ice cubes.

Falconer drank. 'Ah, that's wonderful. Thank you so much, Kerry. We've been drowning in tea and coffee all day, with nothing but a glass or two of squash at lunchtime to cool us down.'

He didn't stay long, but realised that his visits were enjoyed, whether because he was the boss or because he was who he was, he had no idea, but it always boosted his ego when people – with the exception of little Harriet this time – were pleased to see him.

Chapter Eight

Sunday Morning

As Rev. Florrie processed down the aisle, she found she could not sing the words of the hymn, and everything in front of her was viewed through a blur of tears. The crucifer's head was watery and wet, and the rest of the church appeared to be drowned in her tears. She tried to pull herself together; after all, she hadn't really known the man, she only knew what she had been told.

Then she saw that a bouquet of the flowers that had been used to decorate the church had been placed on his usual seat in the choir stalls, and the tears escaped and tracked down her cheeks. Why she felt so emotional, she wasn't quite sure, as the man had been ninety-two, but she suspected it was because he hadn't died a natural death, and also it brought back memories of what had happened in her previous parish.

The bishop had moved her here for a fresh start and now things were happening all over again. It simply wasn't fair, and it was an absolute bummer for old Albert who, it sounded, had never done harm to another living soul, apart from his unfortunate bottom-pinching habit (except, maybe, in the war).

The procession reached its destination and the different elements of it split to take their places for the service, crucifer to abandon his cross and sit where the tenors did by tradition, thurifer to stand in front of the altar, the remainder of the members of the choir into the right hand stalls, and the vicar slightly to the front of everybody else so that she could address the congregation.

She managed to blurt the next hymn number, slightly ahead of schedule, and used the verses to pull herself together, so that she could speak without breaking down. Finally, she began her first address in this new church which, now that her vision had cleared, she was gratified to find fairly full.

This could have been out of respect for the deceased head chorister or sheer ghoulishness, but she liked to think that it was in gratitude in having a new full-time vicar again, even if it was a woman. She had not come across a lot of disapproval and, for this, she was grateful. They could have given her a much harder ride: long may it continue.

When she had recovered her composure, she noticed that whenever the words 'Jesus Christ' were uttered, there was a lot of head bowing and genuflecting, alerting her to the fact that here was very High Church indeed. It was definitely Anglo-Catholic, which was just as well, as that was what she was used to, and she didn't want to put her foot in it if that was not the norm here.

At the end of the service, coffee was served at the back of the church by the font, and quite a few people usually stayed behind for a bit of a natter and a catch up. By chance, she found herself standing next to Polly Garfield, and their conversation, naturally, turned to Friday's tragedy. 'Lost a member of the choir already,' stated Polly in jest, then looked, aghast, as Florrie's eyes filled with tears again.

'I didn't mean anything by it. I was only making conversation. I'm sorry,' she explained.

'Don't be. It's me. I seem to have been very moved by the old man's death, but it's partly what happened before that's adding to the way I feel,' replied the vicar.

'You came over from Shepford St Bernard, didn't

you?' asked Polly, but it was a rhetorical question. Everyone knew that she had, and the events that had taken place there when she had first taken up her position. 'Did anyone tell you that he was robbed a couple of years ago?'

'No. What was taken?' Florrie was horrified. What could Albert have had that anyone would want to steal? She knew where he lived because she had escorted Chelsea home on Saturday morning, and she didn't think he could have much of value in his little cottage.

'His war medals,' Polly informed her.

'How despicable. How can people be so heartless and greedy?'

'They broke in when he was at his ninetieth birthday party at the pub,' Polly concluded.

Rev. Florrie, disgusted and shocked, was absolutely speechless with rage.

Sunday Evening

The vicar had been unable to lock up herself that morning, as she had to get home to accommodate a visit from non-church-going parents about the baptism of their daughter. Wouldn't they be surprised when she told them she only did baptisms as part of a regular Sunday service, as the child would be officially entering the family of the church?

She had, however, asked Yvonne Pooley if she'd see to the doors, as she wanted to practise the new anthem the choir were learning, so that she didn't have to think about her fingers, and could just concentrate on the harmony parts. Florrie was sure she'd do it properly, as she had so many times before, and there was no Evensong there tonight.

It was not a well-attended service generally, although one of her favourites, but was held in rotation round the churches that came under Rev. Monaghan – what a nightmare he was – and tonight it was the turn of Carsfold itself, where the uncomfortable gentleman lived. Just in case he decided to take a drive out afterwards, though, she decided to go down to the church just to have another good poke around. She thought she'd seen something interesting under the sink in the vestry, but hadn't had time to look properly before.

She went into the church, switching the lights on as she did so, then made her way up to the chancel to access the vestry from that entrance. She didn't make it that far, though. Her attention was immediately drawn to the figure seated at the organ in a wooden-backed chair. The sight made her blood freeze and she averted her gaze, but she had to turn round again soon. It was her responsibility if something had happened in her church.

Yvonne Pooley still sat at the organ, her head hanging backwards over the chair. Slowly, she approached the figure, calling out her name, hoping against all odds that Mrs Pooley had just dozed off in a very unusual position. There was, of course, no answer to her greeting. Oh my goodness, there was something sticking out of her mouth, and something on her nose. What was going on here? thought Rev. Florrie, as she got closer.

As she reached the seat that had been provided by the organist herself for the comfort of her back, she saw that there was a clothes peg on her nose – one of the old-fashioned wooden ones, her brain registered – and that there was screwed up paper in her mouth. A few feet away from the seat was what she thought she had seen under the vestry sink – an old misericord – and there was blood on it.

Putting her hand across her own mouth lest she scream, she fumbled around in her handbag and took out the card that she had been given, which had Falconer's work mobile number on it. This was the second death in her church, and she had spent only a few days in the parish.

The inspector was on call, and so his phone was switched

on when she rang the number. Answering it, it took him the best part of a minute to calm down the, by now, almost hysterical vicar. 'Take a couple of deep breaths, Florrie, then start at the beginning, and tell me slowly,' he encouraged her.

'There's another dead body in the church,' she told him, stretching out each word so that she didn't lose control again. 'I came down here, as we don't have Evensong this week, to have another look around: I thought I'd spotted something tucked away in the vestry, and I was right.

'Our choir mistress and organist, Yvonne Pooley, stayed behind after this morning's service to practise after everyone had left, and I just left her to it, as she's got a key. And there she was, still sitting at the instrument, but dead. It was absolutely horrible. There's a blood-stained misericord at her feet, a wooden clothes peg on her nose, and her mouth is full of paper – all of which I didn't touch, by the way.'

'Good girl. Lock the doors and go home if you like, and Carmichael and I will be there as soon as we can.'

As there was absolutely nothing they could do from Market Darley, he rang Carmichael and suggested that he pick him up, and that they arrive together. Castle Farthing was on the way for the inspector, and it would save petrol, even if it was for the police budget.

The two of them were at the vicarage in just over twenty minutes, Falconer having indulged in a bit of over-the-speed-limit driving, with the excuse that if a police car should appear on such a little used route, he could plead that he was on his way to the scene of a crime and that time was of the essence.

He sounded his horn, and Rev. Florrie looked out a window, caught sight of the very distinctive car, and came out of the front door to make her way to the church. No room for a third in a two-seater, especially when one of them was the gigantic Carmichael.

By the time he'd locked his car, Rev. Florrie was already unlocking the church door. She, too, must have been conscious of budget, because she had turned off the lights before she went home. Switching them on again, she just pointed towards the chancel, and sat down in the back pew nearest the door.

The scene was just as she'd described, and Falconer wondered out loud what Doc Christmas would make of this one. He'd alerted him, and requested a team to search the scene, but that wouldn't happen for a little while yet. Doc Christmas would probably be next on the scene, as he seemed to love a good murder. He certainly conducted his post mortems with grisly enthusiasm.

'We'll just have to leave everything until it's been photographed and dusted for prints, but we can get a closer look at what was stuffed in her mouth, and possibly identify it.'

'It's music, sir,' declared Carmichael, whose eyesight was first class.

'So it is,' agreed Falconer, leaning in for a closer look.

'And it looks like it was torn from this book, sir,' said Carmichael, indicating the organist's copy of the *English Hymnal* still present, but now not complete. 'I wonder who would do such a bizarre thing?'

'Somebody making a point, is the only answer that comes to mind. There's some sort of message in this, otherwise why wouldn't whoever did it have cleared up after themselves?'

'Somebody else coming into the building?'

'Possibly, but if the organist had the keys, the murderer would probably have recovered them from her body and locked up again, so as not to attract any suspicion that something had happened here. It definitely looks like a message to me, but what the hell does it mean?'

'No idea, sir, but we might learn more after forensics

have given the place a going over. You're presuming that whoever did this knew that she had the keys in the first place.'

'Well, it was unlikely to be a passing homicidal maniac, was it?'

'I suppose not. That would be rather ridiculous, wouldn't it?'

'Definitely. Let's just hope that they left her like that because they suddenly felt squeamish at what they'd done and wanted to just make a run for it,' replied Falconer.

'Man or woman? What do you think now, sir?'

'Well, the first murder was certainly done with some training and strength in the arms and hands, and the knock over the head with the misericord would have taken a measure of strength too so, for now, I'm going to plump for a man.'

'A man with a clothes peg about his person?' asked Carmichael.

'Anybody who goes about with a clothes peg either has murderous intent or is a bit soft in the head, and that goes for either sex, Sergeant. OK, Florrie, let's get your statement taken, so that you can get off back to the vicarage and, probably a stiff night cap and an early night.'

Chapter Nine

Monday

The inspector caught up with DC Roberts first thing Monday morning, and remembered to ask him what was taken in the burglary of his home, previously his mother's before her early death, not long after the policeman had transferred down from the Manchester force.

'They didn't take much. What I heard were them knocking something off the mantelpiece, and I was out of the shower like a shot. They got the carriage clock and a pair of silver candlesticks. There was probably some cash lying around too: it doesn't matter when you live alone, but I can't really remember.' Typical Roberts, thought Falconer.

'Have they decided whether the graffiti was done at the same time, or the night before?' he asked the young officer.

'They think, because the paint was still wet when I found it' – he hadn't mentioned this during his phone call to the office – 'that it was done before he tried the back door.'

Conscious that the DC had mentioned getting a transfer back to where he'd come from, Falconer didn't call him out on this, merely asking if he'd given any more thought to returning to his previous force. 'I've sort of put it on hold. If I can keep out of hospital or off the sick list for long enough, I can work out how I feel about working here.'

'You haven't had much luck in that department so far, have you?'

'Absolutely not, but I'll just leave the idea on the back burner. What do you want me to do today? I've got myself up to speed on what's happened, including that nasty business last night.'

'Collect PC Green and get yourselves off to Ford Hollow, and do a door to door enquiry about both Friday evening and any time after Sunday service until after dark. It's not a big place, so the two of you can get round it quite easily.'

'Yes, g ... sir,' replied Roberts, who still had trouble not using the hated title 'guv', when addressing the DI.

'Go on, beat it, or I'll let Carmichael loose on your packed lunch.'

Roberts beat it.

By Tuesday they had the first of the forensic reports and the result of the post mortem. Yvonne Pooley had, indeed, been killed by being knocked unconscious with the discarded misericord, then her nose been blocked by the application of the peg, while the sheets of the hymnal stuffed in her mouth had effectively smothered her. Doc Christmas didn't believe she had choked. Time of death: sometime between eleven and three.

There were, of course, a plethora of fingerprints, which would have to be matched up with those who could have handled the misericord, peg, and hymnal innocently and with no murderous intent. No other clue had come to light.

DC Roberts had finished his little break in Ford Hollow by now, and PC Merv Green was back to his usual beat. The only way forward, however, in Falconer's opinion, was to take the fingerprints of anyone who could have had access to these three objects. It probably wasn't the whole village, but it would be a good way of keeping the DC busy, and with a more stern eye on him in the form of the experienced and no-nonsense PC.

'Do I have to, sir?' whined Roberts, when the inspector broke the news to him.

'Of course you do. You know that detection is tedious and repetitive, but it's the only way to get at the solution of a case. You have my permission to go to The Plume of Feathers for your lunch, though.'

'That'll be a bundle of laughs, with a uniform in tow, won't it? I'll have my packed lunch in the car. It's not only cheaper, but it'll be a darned sight less hostile, I reckon.'

'Off you go, Roberts. It's a dirty job, but someone's got to do it.'

Roberts and Green left in a marked police car, the DC sure that people were sick of the sight of them in the village, Green secretly gleeful that Falconer had found this way of keeping the young backslider on the job, and not sloping off all the time for a quick fag and a read of the paper.

Wednesday was the day that the Mothers' Union met, and they usually met at the vicarage, as did the PCC. For some reason (!), there was no church or village hall for them to use, so Rev. Florrie had to prepare herself for another barrage of parishioners wanting tea or coffee and biscuits.

She'd gone to the Brownies' meeting the day before and introduced herself to Brown Owl and the girls. They seemed a nice bunch, and she realised that she would probably know quite a few members of the MU, having already done some visits, been visited, and conducted a service, so it shouldn't be too much of a trial. She didn't have to stay for the meeting itself, and could just look after seating and refreshments.

The meeting was due to start at seven-thirty, and the doorbell went at a quarter past. Assuming it was someone arriving early, she threw open the door, only to find Rev. Monaghan grinning on the doorstep. 'What do you want?'

she asked brusquely, pushing the door until it was nearly closed and applying the security chain. She'd been through enough since she arrived here, and didn't want to find herself the wrong side of his wandering hands again.

'I just wanted to tell you how sorry I was to hear about Mrs Pooley, and to let you know that I really feel for you after what has happened in the short time you've been here.'

You mean you want the opportunity to feel me again, Florrie thought, peering through the tiny gap between door and frame.

'Why have you put on the security chain?' he asked, but before she had managed to manufacture a plausible answer, Sylvia Slater's voice sounded as she approached the vicarage door.

'Are you expecting us, Vicar?' she queried, peering over Rev. Monaghan's shoulder.

'Of course, I am, Sylvia. Rev. Monaghan was just leaving. Weren't you?' she more or less commanded.

'I was. I only called to pass on my condolences,' he lied smarmily.

'Have you called on Mr Pooley and the children yet?' the vicar asked him

'No,' he replied.

'Well, may I suggest that it might be them that need your support now, and not me? It's they who have lost a wife and mother. I have lost an organist, and I have a spare.' Anger made her rather more blunt than she would normally have been, and she heard Sylvia draw in her breath sharply with shock at what appeared to be a very callous remark.

When she'd finally got rid of Monaghan, she invited Sylvia Slater in, and told her why she had reacted so badly. 'I thought you were having a bit of trouble when I saw the chain. We call him Old Bells and Smells, because it was him who made us High Church, and he stinks to high heaven usually. And if he breathes on you, you feel like you're going to pass out. Have you noticed that he always stands too close when he talks to you, and invades your personal space?'

'You know, you're right, Sylvia. I've always felt uncomfortable around him, even though I haven't met him that many times. He gets right in your face, doesn't he?'

'He does, that. And he's a terrible womaniser. Had loads of affairs, and his wife was going to leave him, but the bishop wouldn't support her, and he's got her up the duff again. That'll be her fifth, and the others so grown-up she thought she really had an opportunity to get away from him, but that's scuppered that idea, unless she decides to go it alone, and I can't see how she'd survive.'

'That's disgraceful. Whatever was the bishop thinking about, taking his side, if his behaviour's been that out of order?'

'Men stick together like glue. Men of the cloth stick together like superglue. You'd better believe it,' explained Sylvia, sourly.

'I'm so glad you arrived early. Come on in, and we'll wait for the others together.'

It was only five minutes before the other members started to arrive, and soon there were over a dozen women sitting on chairs of various vintages and designs in the sitting room waiting for the speaker to begin her talk and demonstration which, tonight, was on how to make artificial flowers from an old pair of tights, and the fashioning of carnations from tissue paper.

When Rev. Florrie found out what they were going to be doing, she decided to drag down her dressing table stool and join in. It sounded quite fun, and it would be something to do that would enable her to manufacture small displays for church sales.

Luckily she had plenty of little tables that people could share to hold their materials, and everyone had been asked to bring along a pair of scissors and an old pair of tights or stockings.

The speaker provided the wire that they would need for this first task, and painstakingly went through the process of making each petal, to enable the less nimble-fingered to get the hang of it. While her pupils were fumbling with the task, she made enough petals with her frequent re-demonstrations to make at least three flowers.

Then it was time to fix them together with a rolled and cut paper centre, inserting a wire for the stem. Again, she worked slowly, knowing that people learned in different ways. Some needed to be told what to do. Others needed a drawing or diagram, or a hand-out which she had brought along, and some needed to be physically shown.

It was evident that she had done these demonstrations to many groups in the past, as she was an excellent and patient teacher, and Florrie realised that she would now be inundated with home-made masterpieces for her sales in the future, and her winter evenings were again free. When everyone had produced something that at least vaguely resembled a flower, the speaker told them about dying the tights first to get different colours, and suggested different things that could be used for the centre of the flower. To finish off, she gave them each a length of gutta-percha to produce a finished-looking green stem, at which point Florrie went out into the kitchen to organise the refreshments, having taken everyone's order.

She put on three kettles, being well aware of the thirstiness of parishioners, and raided her crockery cupboard for sufficient mugs, cups, and saucers, to provide for peoples' different tastes. She had bought three packets of biscuits for the evening, again to give the members choice, and everyone would contribute forty pence to be left in a saucer by the trays, to cover her costs.

Having left the doors open, she was able to tune into their conversation now she wasn't in the room with them.

With her present, they tended to be on their best behaviour but, with her out of sight, she was out of mind too, and the buzz of conversation soon rose in volume and the subject turned to the recent murders in the church.

It was Sylvia Slater's voice that declared confidently and, seemingly, knowledgeably, that Yvonne Pooley had been killed by someone from Landbank Ltd, to stop her scuppering their hopes of gaining planning permission to develop the land they had bought from the old farmer.

Others disagreed. Polly Garfield was certain it was a member of the planning committee who had been 'bunged' a bribe, and had either done it himself, or hired someone to do it for him. 'Has anyone spoken to her husband, to see if she ever had any threats by mail or by computer?' This was in Elodie Sutherland's refined tones, adding, 'Any mail would of course have to have been anonymous, unless they were a hundred per cent certain that they had adequately covered their tracks.'

'What about old Albert, then?' asked Thea Scardifield. 'It couldn't have been Landbank Ltd or a member of the planning committee who did for him. He had nothing to do with the protest, did he?'

'That's true, but I reckon it was some old German soldier that Albert had taken prisoner during the war. A lot of them stayed on after the war, and this could be one that wanted to do for Albert before he fell off his perch himself.' Polly Garfield had taken centre stage again, only to be superseded by Elodie Sutherland.

'My mother said that Albert was little more than a boy when he joined up..'

'What's that got to do with the price of eggs?' asked Marjorie Mundy, who had remained silent up till now, but now unleashed her waspish side. 'I reckon it was Thea's husband Willard, because he wanted the organist's position. He is second-in-command, after all, where that wheezy decrepit beast is concerned.'

'How could you even suggest such a thing?' asked Thea Scardifield, suddenly full of rage. 'Willard wouldn't hurt a fly, and I resent that suggestion strongly.'

Having heard the way the conversation was going, Rev. Florrie made her appearance in the doorway with her loaded tray, put it down, and went back to the kitchen for the other one, before finally collecting the biscuits and sugar bowl. Her appearance had calmed down things considerably, though, and she had made a note of everything that had been said, and was now looking forward to the making of paper carnations.

The demonstration was, again, utterly engrossing and a lot of fun. The speaker showed them how to roll the paper and secure it with a wire that would then become the stem, then make several cuts down it, before fluffing it out almost flat to make an object that was not, even by now, unlike a carnation.

The next step was to wrap a little piece of paper round where it was secured to make the shape from which the bud opens, and wrap the wire with another length of gutta-percha.

'If you want to,' she said, removing a small tablet bottle from her handbag, and removing her saucer from under her cup before pouring into it a reddish liquid, 'you can just dip the very ends of your flower in something like red ink, and you get the effect of a very fine ribboning to give a more realistic look. If anyone wants to do that, they're welcome to come up and dip their efforts into my saucer.'

All the women queued like well-trained school-children to do this, even Florrie joining the end of the line, and that was the end of the meeting. Thea Willard, who arranged the speakers for each monthly meeting, raised her voice above the sound of mugs, cups, and saucers being loaded back on to trays and the sound of chairs being returned to their original place, to announce that next month she had somebody coming to show them how to make their own Christmas crackers, so that they would have plenty of time to get 'cracking' before the festive season and, perhaps, give some of them out as seasonal gifts.

As she carried a heavy old wooden chair back to the dining room Florrie reckoned that she would attend that meeting as well, and thought that she would thoroughly enjoy the MU meetings, which she had originally thought would be a bit of a bore, and not to her taste at all. As she came back into the hall, Polly Garfield sidled up to her and said she wouldn't be surprised if Thea didn't fancy the position of choir mistress herself. That way, she and Willard would have the whole of the church music sewn up between them.

'Don't be such a gossip, Polly. I'm sure that's only a rumour by somebody who's jealous of their musical ability.'

'Do you think so, Vicar?'

'I'm sure of it,' replied Florrie, but when they had all gone and she was left on her own, she was not so sure. There were so many rumours started maliciously, and so much patently untrue gossip, but there may well have been something in what the women were suggesting tonight and, late though it was, she determined to ring Inspector Falconer and tell him of the ideas that had been aired tonight.

Chapter Ten

Thursday

Falconer positively bustled into the office the morning after his phone call from Rev. Florrie. The work in the office so far had been concentrated on sifting through the statements given by villagers, but her information had sparked off new ideas. Villagers mostly kept their innermost thoughts to themselves, when questioned by outsiders, and the ideas she had given him had sparked off a lot of new theories, each of which he was going to run past Carmichael, who was a few minutes behind his normal arrival time.

'Sorry, sir,' called a voice from the door. 'Had a bit of bother in the bathroom.'

'Whatever do you mean?' asked Falconer, turning round sufficiently that his eyes explained all. His sergeant was newly Scandinavian blond. 'What the hell happened?'

'A moment's inattention,' he said, flopping into a chair and running a hand through his newly pale hair. 'Kerry called me down when I'd just got out of the shower, and I grabbed what I thought was my hair gel tube. I put it on, not bothering with the mirror in my hurry, ran a comb through it, and belted downstairs.

'Kerry was really upset, because she'd gone out to feed the chickens, and found one of them dead. When I got there, she rushed indoors crying and asked me to get rid of it, then she went upstairs for a good howl. When she came down again, she just said, "What the hell have you done,

Davey?" and I looked at her with no idea what she meant.

'She told me to go look in a mirror, then get myself back in the shower as quick as I could. I'd grabbed her hair colour by mistake,' he explained ruefully. 'She said that if I didn't condition it within an inch of its life it'd blow up like a dandelion clock and frizz out, and there was no way I fancied a blond afro.' Only Carmichael could have made such a mistake, thought the inspector, and asked him what he could do about it.

'Not much I could do. Kerry said I basically have three options. I could try to tough it out looking like this, which might be tricky. Secondly, I could have my head shaved, and thirdly, I could let it grow a bit, then have it cut short, so that I have what are known as "blond tips".'

'And which option do you favour?' asked Falconer now interested to discover the workings of his sergeant's mind.

'Not sure, sir,' came the reply. 'I'm going to give it some thought during the day.'

'Well, don't dwell on it too much. I've got some information from Rev. Florrie, which has given us at least one good lead, maybe two. The third one was too ridiculous to contemplate – but then, so was what you did first thing this morning, so I suppose we'll have to look into it too. The work will keep your mind off what you look like.'

'Don't make fun of me, sir. Bob Bryant gave me a wolf-whistle when I came in, and Merv Green blew a kiss at me and called me Blondie,' pleaded the sergeant with a crestfallen expression.

'You just wait until you get to the canteen, then the fun will really start. You'd better put on your thickest skin before we go there.'

'Don't, sir,' wailed Carmichael, his face falling even further. 'I would avoid the place for a while, but I need my food.'

'You surely do.'

'Now, what are these leads you got, and when did you get them?'

'Rev. Florrie hosted her first Mothers' Union meeting last night, and those hens did cackle when she went into the kitchen to make them a hot drink. The most ludicrous one is that an old German soldier from the war who was taken prisoner by Albert has come after him before he dies. I know it sounds ludicrous, but it could be a son or grandson who decided to pay the old man back. If his relative had a bad time or even died, he might have thought there were grounds for revenge.'

'It's a bit of a long shot, sir,' said Carmichael, looking amazed that such a thing could have been suggested.

'I know, but we can check Burton's war record, and also check if anyone knows of a German visiting the area. It's the least we can do, although I think it very unlikely.

'The second theory that I'm going to pass on to you is that the Scardifields did away with Yvonne Pooley, because Willard wanted to be appointed organist, and Thea wanted to take over running the choir. I know it sounds a bit outrageous, but murder has been done for less, and, if you remember, they did say they were going away, so maybe they were going to their daughter's, or wherever they've gone, to let things cool down a bit and see if they've got away with it.

'We also need to have a good talk with Mr Pooley to see if his wife ever had any anonymous threats. They could've been delivered by post, been pushed through the door, or sent by e-mail. The computer she used will tell us about electronic threats, but anything in paper form might have been destroyed, but I bet she would've told her husband.

'And that ties in very much with the third suggestion: that someone from Landbank Ltd, the company that has sold off the land they bought from the abandoned farm, might have done away with her to stop her protest scuppering their plans to get the development off the ground. Maybe they're being badgered already by investors wanting an idea of when they'll see a return on their money.'

'Now, that sounds like quite a sensible theory, sir.'

'And, it was suggested that it might have been someone from the local planning committee who had been bribed to see it through to approval. Yvonne Pooley must have been a bit of a fly in the ointment.'

'Morning, sir, Carmichael,' called Roberts' voice from the door. 'I've finished everything up in Ford Hollow. What do you want me on today? Got anything juicy?'

'Ah, just the man,' declared Falconer, with a wolfish grin. 'I want you to get the names, addresses, and telephone numbers of all the members on the local planning committee, and the same for anyone in a position of seniority in the planning department itself. And by the way, you're late – again.'

Roberts' cheerful expression melted away, and he scowled at the inspector. 'Gee whizz, thanks a bundle, sir. From one desert to another. I shall really enjoy that.'

'Of course you will. It's real police work. No car chases, and no weapons, just good solid investigative footwork. And don't moan. You can probably get a lot of it either on the phone or on the internet. That can't be a bad option, can it, sitting on your backside away from all the baddies. By the way, I hope you've been locking up diligently since your intruder.'

'Ha ha, sir, very funny, I don't think. Yes I have, and now I'd better get on with my dry as dust work.'

'What do you want me to do?' asked Carmichael.

'I'd like you to check Companies House for a copy of Landbank Ltd's registration, any returns they have made, and a list of the directors.'

'And what are you going to do?' asked Roberts

sarcastically.

'I'm going to wait until Carmichael has some names for me, then he and I are going to do some ringing around to make appointments to see some of the personnel of that particular company.

'We'll probably be out when you've finished, so I wonder if you'd be so good as to write up your case notes for me to sign off when I get back.'

'That's it. I'm definitely transferring back to Manchester.'

'Suit yourself,' replied Falconer, with the very slightest of sneers. Would he miss his DC, or would he be better off with a replacement? At the moment, he really didn't know.

By ten o'clock, Falconer had made appointments for the managing director and the three listed directors of the company, and they left Roberts to his boring tasks, Carmichael delighted that they were getting out of the office, because he wouldn't have to face the canteen at lunchtime.

Falconer had been, somehow, persuaded to go to Landbank Ltd in Carmichael's car. How he could have been so stupid, he did not know, but he could hardly have been surprised when it broke down about a mile before they had even reached Castle Farthing, the company having its registered office in Carsfold.

'Bloody marvellous. I thought you told me a couple of weeks ago that it had passed its MOT, and that it was only visually that it looked a wreck.'

'There were a few things that were going to rear their heads in the near future, but nothing he could call me out on when he certified it.'

'Is he an habitual liar, or was this out of character?' snapped Falconer.

'He must've just miscalculated the timing, sir. He's a very honest man,' replied Carmichael, hurt by this slur on the man's reputation. 'I've used him for years.'

'If he's been giving this old bucket of rust its MOTs for that long, he must be a real crook. I would've insisted it be scrapped years ago.'

'There's nothing wrong with her, sir. Except, obviously, for the fact that she's broken down. She's just a bit ugly, and I can't afford a re-spray.'

'*She*,' replied Falconer, emphasizing the pronoun, which he had never noticed his sergeant using before, 'would not be worth the price of the paint, let alone the labour. In fact, if you sold *her*, I doubt you'd get the price of a fish supper. So, what do we do now?'

'I'll phone the garage, sir,' said his sergeant in a very sulky voice. His face grew even grimmer when he'd made his phone call. 'He can't come to get her before two o'clock. He said to lock her up and leave her. What do we do now?'

'We'll walk to yours, and have an early lunch with Kerry, if you don't think she'd be put out, then we'll get a pool car driven out to us so that we can go on.'

'Great!' That certainly cheered up Carmichael and brought the smile back to his face. 'I'll just lock her up, and we'll get going. Thank goodness it's not raining.'

It was sunny, but by the time they'd collected all their bits and pieces and Carmichael had persuaded the central locking to work – a bit like Russian roulette – dark clouds had obliterated this sign of an Indian summer, and fat drops began to fall on them. 'Didn't you have an umbrella in there?' asked Falconer.

'Sorry, sir. I used it last week to get into the office when we had a shower, and I've left it in there on the coat stand.'

'Bloody marvellous. You could at least phone Kerry and let her know we're coming.'

'It's not my fault it's raining, sir.'

'Yes it is.'

By the time Carmichael dialled the number, the signal, always dicey outside the villages, and sometimes in them, had disappeared, and they began to trudge towards Castle Farthing, with nothing whatsoever to shelter them.

Two things hit Rev. Florrie during the morning. One, when she looked at the list that had been made for her, was the realisation that there was to be a team ministry line dancing evening in Carsfold, which she would be expected to attend. The other was that tomorrow night was choir practice again, and she had no choir mistress.

This called for a cup of real coffee, instead of the decaf she normally drank at home. After a lot of mulling it over, she decided that she would ring Elodie Sutherland. Although the Scardifields weren't going away until Saturday, she didn't want to ask Thea to take the practice, as it would confirm the fears of some of the members of the MU that this really was a plot by the couple to take over the church music in a Mafia-style coup. It would be a rumour quashed, and, she hoped, not just for now. Weirder reasons had been given for doing murder so often in the past that she just hoped she was doing the right thing.

Elodie was, of course, delighted to oblige. Although she tried to sound like she was doing the vicar a favour, it was obviously the vicar who had made the woman's day. Right, that was that out of the way. Now for some thought about the evening.

She immediately rang Marjorie Mundy to see if she was going, and was secretly delighted when the old woman said yes. She wasn't exactly of the desired size or fitness for the line dancing, but she went to as many parish dos as she could just to observe. It gave her a lot of innocent amusement. 'In that case, could I sit with you? I don't want to be cornered by the dreadful Rev. Monaghan again. He really gives me the creeps.'

'You and every other woman not already in the grave,

in all of his parishes. He's an absolute menace, and I wish the bishop would move him but, for some reason, those two seem to be great buddies. You know about his wife, don't you?'

They spent the next ten minutes blackening the reverend sinner's name and feeling sorry for his poor wife. 'Mind you, I expect something very surprising will happen there someday,' said Marjorie.

'You don't think she'll murder him, do you?'

'You just mark my words. She's going to surprise us all.'

By the time that Falconer and Carmichael got to Jasmine Cottage, they were soaked to the skin. Kerry opened the door looking even more rounded than she had a few days ago, if that were possible, and hurried them inside.

'You get yourself upstairs and change, Davey, while I find Inspector Falconer something clean of yours to put on, so that I can put both lots of clothes in the tumble drier.'

Falconer nearly had a conniption at the thought of his trousers in the jaws of a tumble drier, and asked her if she would plug her iron in, and he would iron them dry. But not until he had something to cover his embarrassment, by which she supposed he meant his legs and underpants. He was hardly the sort of person to go commando.

Falconer stood in the kitchen and dripped as he waited for Kerry to come back with a change of clothes. She was first of the couple to reappear, and handed him a T-shirt and a pair of jogging bottoms. Thanking her, he went upstairs himself to the modesty of the bathroom to change out of his drowned garments.

When he had put them on, he looked down at himself and sighed. This was inevitably what would happen. The full-length mirror on the landing wall confirmed what he had already decided. He looked like he had shrunk in the wash. The T-shirt hung off his shoulders and halfway down his arms, and the body of it reached nearly to his knees. And did it have to be in black and yellow horizontal stripes? He looked like a giant bee, but felt more like an angry wasp, waiting for a victim to sting.

The jogging bottoms also pooled around his feet over the elasticated ankles, and when he heard the handle of Carmichael's bedroom door turn, he was ready for him, his stinger poised to strike.

What he saw froze the words in his throat. Whereas the jogging bottoms he had been lent were grey, Carmichael's were a startling turquoise. Even his T-shirt outdid the one Falconer was wearing, being a violent shade of hot pink, with purple trim at the neck, shoulders, and along the bottom.

'I hope you're only wearing those while your other clothes dry?' he asked, in a rather high-pitched voice, wondering what the directors and managing director of a company would think of a plain clothes policeman dressed in such bright raiment.

'If Kerry can get them dry in time. If not, I don't really have any other grown-up clothes that aren't either in the wash or at the dry cleaner's.'

'Well, I hope to God that she can get them ready for wear. I don't fancy trolling you round a company's registered office in that get up.'

'What's wrong with it, sir? It's not quite autumn and I thought it was cheerful.'

'It might cheer you up, but it fills me with dread. Come on, let's get downstairs. I told Kerry she could tumble-dry my shirt before ironing it, but I shall have to iron my own trousers and tie dry. I can't let them go in that instrument of garment torture.'

When they got back downstairs, the churning of the offending machine could be heard, and there were two plates of sandwiches on the table, along with two mugs of tea. As they sat down, Kerry asked, 'What do you think of Davey's hair? Isn't he a plonker?'

'I'd say so, Kerry, but I think his outfit rather goes with it. It's just a pity that I wouldn't like to be seen out in public with him dressed like that, and I can hardly get him to wear a hat as well. No doubt he'd produce a lime green one.'

'I could wear a baseball cap, sir.'

With memories of what Carmichael used to look like when he wore just such an item of headgear regularly, Falconer replied, 'Oh, no you couldn't. I absolutely forbid it.'

'A headscarf, then?'

'Carmichael, please don't make me cross. You wouldn't like me when I'm angry.'

'Oh!' The sergeant's eyes glowed. 'Do you watch *The Incredible Hulk* as well sir?'

'I certainly do not. It was just a turn of phrase, now shut your mouth and eat your sandwiches.'

'Sir?'

'Yes, Carmichael?' asked the inspector, a sandwich halfway to his mouth.

'How do I shut my mouth *and* eat my sandwiches. I wouldn't be able to get them in if my mouth was shut.'

'You know damned well what I mean, sarkie.'

Carmichael grinned at the easy victory, his for once, and tucked in with enthusiasm.

After they had eaten, Kerry made them both another cup of tea while they sat and waited for a car to be delivered from the police station in Market Darley.

Their clothes weren't quite dry, and Falconer, who had commenced ironing even as his hostess had taken away the plates, took a short break to drink. Within a couple of minutes, he had acquired a Chihuahua and a tiny Yorkshire terrier, one along each of his upper legs. Why did they do this? They knew he didn't like dogs, yet they persisted in singling him out for special attention. Waddling over rather late, Dipsy Daxie, the new addition, sat down at his feet and began to chew his shoe laces. He had a full set now – or had he?

At that point, as he was glaring at his three furry fans, glad that it was Carmichael's clothing that he was wearing, there was a knock at the door, and Kerry answered it to what sounded like a couple – and yet another animal. There was a deep *wuff*, and Falconer's blood froze. Oh no, it couldn't be! It surely couldn't be, could it? It mustn't be Mulligan again, thought the inspector, and he hoped they weren't going to come in.

'I'll see you on Sunday night then,' they heard Kerry say, and in trotted – like a horse – the enormous bulk that was Mulligan the Great Dane, one of Falconer's most avid canine fans who had once, against Falconer's will, shared a bed with him.

If dogs could have purred, Mulligan would have been making a noise like a train. Scenting his favourite person, he gave a great howl of joy, and threw himself on to Falconer's lap, the smaller dogs just jumping free in time before they were squashed.

'Isn't that lovely, sir? He still remembers you. I forgot to mention he was coming for a long weekend.'

There was no answer. Mulligan was so large that there was no room for him on one lap, and his sudden arrival on Falconer's had knocked him sideways, the only solution being to try to pull himself up from under so that it at least looked like he was sitting there. But he needed help.

'Don't just drag me out,' he shouted, with as much breath as he could muster. 'Get this monster off me. He's squashing me flat.'

When the car was finally delivered, Mulligan had been ousted to the back garden, where he whined pathetically, begging to come back in to his best friend, Falconer had managed to iron everything dry, but Carmichael's clothes had resisted the efforts of the tumble dryer, and it was only when there was a horn sounded from out in the road, that Kerry noticed that she had left the machine set on low.

'No wonder you had to iron your shirt to get it completely dry,' she said to Falconer, who'd insisted that he do it himself. He ironed his shirts like a soldier, and couldn't bear it when someone else 'made a mess of it', as he thought of it. 'I'd not changed the setting since the last wash, which was for delicates,' Kerry concluded in explanation.

'So I suppose that means I get Ka-Ka the Klown here for company this afternoon.'

'Looks like it, sir,' confirmed Carmichael. He did actually have something else more sober that he could have worn, but he was secretly enjoying baiting the boss and, thus, kept quiet about it. 'Are you going outside to say goodbye to Mulligan?'

'Not on your life!' replied Falconer, physically flinching at the thought.

Chapter Eleven

Thursday afternoon

When they arrived in the car park for the address given for Landbank Ltd, a huge block of offices confronted them. Walking towards it, they felt quite intimidated, until the stares and wolf whistles began from other visitors or members of staff, and Carmichael's face clashed with his clothes for a minute or two.

On reaching the entrance, they could see that the building was occupied by a multiplicity of firms, all probably quite small. Landbank Ltd was indicated as being on the sixth and top floor. The lift was, of course, out of order.

'Are you Zippy, Bungle, George, or Geoffrey?' asked Falconer, only to be presented with a very puzzled face. 'Come along, *Rainbow*,' he clarified, and the sergeant's face cleared, as he finally recognised the reference to an old children's TV programme.

'I think I'll be Geoffrey,' he replied. 'He always wore brightly coloured clothes.'

'If I had my choice, you'd be Zippy,' muttered Falconer, with an evil grin.

After four flights, old Rainbow-Chops was as fresh as a daisy, but Falconer was winded and needed to stop for a rest. 'When's your next official medical, sir?' asked Carmichael, with genuine interest and not a hint of malice.

'In two weeks' time,' answered Falconer, holding on to the bannister and panting. 'I think I'd better get myself off to the gym as soon as possible.'

'It might be an idea, sir. I mean, I can imagine Roberts getting puffed because he smokes and never moves unless he has to, but I'd have thought you would have been fitter.'

'So would I, Sergeant. So would I. Come on, this isn't getting the baby boiled.'

'I think you mean bathed, sir.'

'I mean exactly what I said, Carmichael. Now, let's get up the rest of these blasted stairs, and get on with our first interview, when I've got my breath back.'

There was a row of chairs on the landing at the top of the stairs, and Falconer sank down gratefully into one. 'We've still got five minutes, so we can wait until I'm a little less breathless,' he said. However, it was not to be, and his voice must have carried into the one office he wouldn't have wanted it to; that of the managing director.

A figure burst out of the door, took one look at them and said, 'Police. I'm ready for you. Come in. I'm Cardew Trevelyan, by the way. Title as on the sign on the door.'

Carmichael stood up, his full height, and the complete colour scheme on show, Trevelyan took a step back, and only recomposed himself when they had both shown him their warrant cards.

Falconer hauled himself to his feet and followed Carmichael into the office. When all three had taken their seats, Falconer made a brief apology for his colleague's attire, then continued, 'The reason we're here' – puff puff – 'is to talk to you about' – huff puff – 'Mrs Yvonne Pooley.' The effort of this had evidently exhausted him, and Carmichael got out his notebook and took over.

'We understood that she was getting up a petition to halt the development at Ford Hollow, and that she had been very vociferous in her protests.'

Trevelyan's features had screwed themselves into an angry little ball at the mention of the woman's name, and his reply was quite explosive. 'Bloody woman! Does she know how many jobs, how many livelihoods are at stake over a development like this? And the pressure on housing is getting even stronger. Land that is dead agriculturally should be able to be re-zoned easily into ground for building.'

'Aren't you afraid that the homes you build will flood?' asked Falconer, now virtually recovered.

'Why should they if they divert the stream that flows through the perimeter? And anyway, we won't be building them, just getting planning permission and selling the land on to a developer.'

'Then the village wouldn't have a ford,' interrupted Carmichael.

'Correct.'

'So how could it be called Ford Hollow any more? It doesn't make sense,' continued the sergeant.

'That's not my concern. I'm not in the least interested what they call the place – they can call it Cloud Cuckoo Land, as far as I'm concerned – as long as I can get a return for my investors, and get the thing moved on past Planning and see it go into building.'

'But surely your financial interest finishes after you've sold on the tiny plots?'

'Not at all. Not only do we guarantee to be guardians of the land until it does sell on, but we have retained certain plots for ourselves, so that when it has planning permission and is bought by a developer, we get a new injection of capital to fund future land purchases.

'And was Mrs Pooley a bit of a fly in the ointment.'

'She is an enormous nuisance,' he replied, not initially noticing the past tense, 'constantly writing to her MP, the local council, us, putting together petitions and lobbying green groups.' Now the penny dropped. 'You said "was".'

'Unfortunately Mrs Pooley was murdered last Sunday. That's the reason we've come to see you and your colleagues today. We have appointments with the three directors listed at Companies House. Could you tell me how many other staff you have?'

'None.'

'There are only four of you?'

'That's all we need. One of the directors is a surveyor to sniff out plots of land available, one an architect, to work out how many homes we would be looking at for planning permission. The other takes care of sales.'

'And what do you do?'

'I mostly do the book-keeping. If we had any more staff we'd never make a profit. We run as a very mean, lean machine.'

'And does that meanness stretch as far as murdering anyone who stirs up trouble for you?'

'Absolutely not. We'd probably have tried to buy her off.'

'What about your colleagues? Do you know what they're doing twenty-four hours a day?'

'No, but they'd never resort to murder,' said Trevelyan, still shocked at the very suggestion that Yvonne Pooley's death could have anything to do with his firm.

'We'll make up our own minds, as I've made appointments to see them all. Thank you for your help.' Falconer rose, and he and Carmichael left the room in search of the other directors' offices.

The next one along was signed for a Sheridan Grimble, and Falconer knocked, trying to hide Carmichael with his body, and disconcerted when the sergeant moved to stand beside him. When the occupant of the office opened the door, there was a moment of silence that seemed to go on forever.

The man's nose was so enormous and misshapen, it looked like he didn't own a sock drawer and had shoved them up there with nowhere else to keep them. To add to his odd appearance, he wore a pair of horn-rimmed glasses and a very thick moustache bristling just above his upper lip. Both Grimble and Carmichael broke the embarrassing silence by bursting into laughter simultaneously. Hastily trying to smother their mirth, Carmichael's at the enormous 'schconk' and its accoutrements, Grimble's at Carmichael's 'plain clothes', it was Falconer who was the one that was most embarrassed, and he remained a sunburnt crimson until they were all seated in the office.

Sensing the subject of the sergeant's mirth, he kept fingering his misshapen hooter as he inspected their warrant cards, making Falconer prickle all over his body with shame at Carmichael's uncalled for mirth. Carmichael was incapable of embarrassment as far as his dress went, and just sat there staring, fascinated by the size of the facial organ he saw before him.

The inspector cut straight to the chase. 'What do you know about Yvonne Pooley from the village of Ford Hollow?' Carmichael was too busy surveying the contents of the office space, which included a huge drawing board with a set of plans displayed on it. Here was, obviously, the architect of the company.

Grimble was somewhat slow in replying. 'Nothing,' he finally ventured, and a slight look of apprehension washed over his features, having to make quite a detour to take in his nose as well.

'Nothing, Mr Grimble? But surely she's been making life very difficult for Landbank Ltd lately?'

'I know the name,' he admitted, reluctantly.

'You've never met her in person?' asked Falconer. It took quite a while for a denial to be offered, and Grimble avoided the inspector's eye as he made it. 'Are you absolutely sure of that? Has she ever been here?'

'No comment,' intoned Grimble in a monotone.

'Are you refusing to answer my question?'

'No comment.'

They left Grimble's office shortly afterwards, able to

get nothing further from him but no comment.

Once outside again, Falconer declared, 'There's something fishy about that man. He's definitely got something to hide. We may have to take him in to be questioned and, no doubt, he'll yell for his solicitor like a child for its nanny.'

Carmichael knew nothing of nursery nannies, associating the word, instead, with grandmothers, and innocently nodded his agreement, then adding, 'But you've got to admit he looks a lot like Groucho Marx. I bet that nose and the moustache are attached to the glasses, and he takes the whole thing off at night and put them on the bedside table until he needs them again the next morning.' It was a charming flight of fantasy, and quite inventive for the sergeant.

'He had a painted moustache,' replied the inspector.

'What, Grimble? Was it really?

'No, Groucho Marx, you fool.'

'Oh. So Grimble's is real?'

'Of course it is. How could it be false?'

'They do some very convincing false moustaches these days. Look at the Poirot programmes,' advised the sergeant, happy to go along with this different reality.

'I shall do no such thing, Carmichael. Why on earth would the man wear a false moustache?'

'Disguise?'

'Oh, grow up.'

The next office had two signs on the door, and was occupied by Xavier Smallwood, who was the surveyor of the company, and Sigmund Aylesford, who took care of sales and negotiating for new land. After warrant cards had been shown, introductions carried out, and all four were seated, Falconer, who had a fascination with scientific instruments, said, 'Mr Smallwood, do you think I could take a look at your theodolite?'

Carmichael hissed, 'Sir! What do you think you're

doing?' then was puzzled as the director got up and went to the back of the office and took a box out of the storage under the window seat. As the man lifted the lid, the sergeant leaned forward, and leaned back again, looking like he had not at all been shown what he thought Falconer was asking to see. So that's what a ... a theo ... one of those things was. He'd thought he'd heard the word 'theodildo', and that would've been something altogether different.

Both men admitted to knowing who Yvonne Pooley was, and Smallwood even admitted to having met her, although he said this was by accident, when he was surveying the land just before the purchase was completed. With a determination to seize all the company's computers to check for poison e-mails, Falconer called Carmichael to heel, and they left them to get on with their work.

Once back on the landing again Falconer asked quietly, 'What's all this with the fancy names: Cardew, Sheridan, Xavier, and Sigmund? Is it just that younger people's parents prefer to name their child something a little different?'

'Well, my mum certainly did,' replied Carmichael lugubriously. 'Remember, I've got brothers called Romeo, Hamlet, Mercutio, and Harry – cry God for Harry and all that rot – and sisters called Juliet and Imogen.'

'How could I forget your brothers? They got me absolutely rat-arsed at your wedding to Kerry, and the lot of them had it in for me at the christening. And, of course, you're Ralph Orsino.'

'Don't rub it in, sir.'

'Your mum certainly had a passion for Shakespeare, didn't she?' grinned Falconer. 'Now, these stairs shouldn't be quite so hard work on the way down.' He hoped. After three flights, he had to take a break again, panting like a broken-winded horse. 'I really don't seem to be at the peak of physical fitness,' he puffed.

'You sound more like a "forty fags a day" old woman,' commented Carmichael, racing down the last two flights.

'That's not very kind,' replied Falconer wheezily and with a glower, setting off after the sergeant, but at a much slower pace.

To the inspector's glee, however, Carmichael picked up quite a collection of wolf-whistles, cat calls, and stares on the way back to the car, and was glad when he could get inside it out of sight, and they could return to Market Darley.

When they got back to the station, Falconer said, as they had been offered no form of refreshment at Landbank Limited's offices, 'Come on, let's go and get coffee and a bun. I think we've earned it.'

'Oh, no! Holy camoly!'

'Whatever's the matter, Carmichael?'

'I meant to stop in and change into my clothes that Kerry was drying. Whatever are they going to say in the canteen?'

'Oh, nothing you can't handle. Come on, let's go and brighten up all the other customers' day for them.'

While Carmichael sat in trepidation at his forthcoming ordeal in the canteen, Roberts claimed to have finished the case notes, except for those that they had to add about their interviews today. 'I'm going for a coffee,' said the DC, getting up slowly and stretching, as if in the search of sympathy for all the hours he had spent hunched over a computer today. It was unforthcoming, and after he left the room, Falconer took a look through what he had recorded. He had not given Carmichael's newly Scandinavian hair and outlandishly colourful get-up a glance.

After a couple of minutes, the inspector put his chin on the palms of his hands and called Carmichael over. Look at this!' he said pointing at the computer screen. 'And this – and that!' Sighing, he waved Carmichael away, and said 'I'll just have to go through the notes myself. The grammar's awful, the punctuation's absolutely dire, and as for the spelling … Look! He's turned the auto-correct off. It's going to take ages – yes, there it goes. I've turned it on now, and nearly everything's underlined in some colour or another. It's almost like a rainbow.'

'Well, I'm not going to that canteen on my own,' stated Carmichael firmly.

'You could've gone with Roberts.'

'No fear. What protection would *he* be? At least *you* can glare at people, and they usually behave better.'

'Then I suggest you write up today's notes while I put this pile of drivel right, and we'll go together.' At this encouragement, Carmichael got out his notebook and sat down in front of his terminal.

'But just remember that I'm not your nanny,' was Falconer's final comment, leaving Carmichael wondering why on earth the inspector thought that he might think of him as his grandmother.

In Ford Hollow Rev. Florrie finally dismissed all the gossip from last night's MU meeting, and phoned the Scardifields. She needed them, Willard to play the organ while Thea took the choir practice. She knew they would not be there on Sunday, but she would deal with that as a separate issue. Her only other choice was Elodie Sutherland, and she knew she would not be able to swallow the smugness of the woman, as she stood at the front of the other choristers, probably behaving like an elderly female tyrant.

Willard accepted for them both quite happily, becoming almost flippant. 'As long as that doesn't mean we get bumped off,' he joked, making Florrie cringe at his bad taste. 'By the way, you know we're not going to be here for Sunday service, don't you? We're going over to France to visit our daughter. And, what's more, I shan't be coming back just to play for the service. See you tomorrow night,' he chirped, and hung up. As far as he was concerned, there were no niceties to be indulged in at the end of a call.

There was nothing more that Florrie could do. What more could happen? If the crucifer fell off his perch, then she'd just have to carry the cross herself. Oh good grief, I've got to get ready quickly, thought Florrie. It's that dratted line dancing tonight in Carsfold, and I'm expected to attend. I hope that clerical octopus keeps his hands to himself, or I won't be responsible for my actions.

Carsfold's St Ignatius Church had its own large hall, being in a small town rather than a very small village, and she set off in her car full of trepidation, hoping to be able to latch on to Marjorie and her cronies, and keep away from old Wandering Hands himself.

She arrived only minutes before Rev. Monaghan began his calling of instructions, and a short line was already forming. All the others were gathered round the punch bowl, absorbing as much as they could from their all-inclusive ticket.

'Come along, now,' shouted Old Bells and Smells. 'Let's get a decent line formed here so that we can get on. Come along all of you. I thought you came here to learn how to line dance?'

Several others lengthened the line, and Florrie was able to slip into a free chair where Mrs Mundy was holding court. 'Glad you could make it,' the old woman wheezed with a smile.

'I nearly didn't.' replied Florrie. 'I only remembered about it at the last minute, and had to rush like billy-o to get here. Is he only just starting?'

'Just getting up his steam. He'll be at it for another two hours or more, just you wait and see. He never seems to get hoarse or breathless. Must keep a tank of oxygen hidden in his beard: there's certainly room for one.'

Placed around a few tables were hard wooden chairs,

the majority of the seating having been lined up against the walls to give the dancers more room. 'Just look at them,' said Marjorie. 'In their twinsets and pearls and identical perms, they look like they've either been stuffed or recently exhumed. What are you having for supper tonight?'

'Pollock,' answered the vicar truthfully.

'I know it was a nosy question, but I didn't expect to get an answer like that,' replied Mrs Mundy, then smiled at Florrie's crestfallen face.

'No, I didn't mean that. The fish, you know, pollock, not … what you thought I said.'

'I knew what you meant. I was only pulling your leg, but, mind, they can be a very bony fish.'

The buzz of chatter continued below the shouting of Rev. Monaghan, until suddenly it was half-time, and he let them all go, as another full punch bowl was wheeled out on a trolley. 'There!' he called, not waiting to be ignored during this natural break. 'I told you that you wouldn't miss anything by joining in with the line.'

After the bowl had been drained of its last drop of all-inclusive, Monaghan tried to get the line-up and dancing again, this time spotting Rev. Florrie and literally dragging her, by one of his sweaty hands, to join in. 'I'll call from the centre, and we'll all dance one more time through the one we did in the first half. Here, next to me, Rev. Feldman. You missed all the practise we've already had, so you'll need some guiding.'

Florrie did as she was told, reluctantly, as there didn't seem to be any way out of it but, as she felt his hand reach down, when they were all facing their left-hand companions' backs, and caress her left buttock, she'd had enough. Before she could say or do anything, they were asked to about-turn, and she was facing his back, and was suddenly engulfed in a noxious cloud of gas which could only have emanated from Rev. Monaghan.

Before she could get her breath back, they all turned one hundred and eighty degrees again, and now he put a hand on each of her buttocks. With no further ado, she broke the line, turned to face Rev. Monaghan, and slapped him squarely on the chops.

'You can keep your filthy wandering hands to yourself where I'm concerned,' she said, 'And as for your wind problem, I know a very good vet who will prescribe you some charcoal biscuit. I'm going home now, and I shan't be attending any other entertainments which might include you.'

Her face a bright red, she turned away from the line, only to be flabbergasted by the spontaneous round of applause that greeted her rebellion. 'Well said, Vicar,' called one voice.

'You've said it for all us women,' called another, and she left the dancing area a heroine.

'Times have changed, and we simply won't stand for it any more. How do you like them potatoes, Rev. Monaghan?'

Even the men would not speak out in his support, knowing that they would get hell from their wives when they got home if they dared do such a chauvinistic thing. Rev. Monaghan left the hall ignominiously, while those left behind carried on dancing the first set of moves he had taught them and the whole hall declared itself a party zone.

Chapter Twelve

Friday

On Friday morning, Rev. Florrie was summoned to the Sutherland household by a very snotty sounding Elodie who, for once, insisted that she be called Miss Sutherland, and who might just possibly have heard a whisper from the village grapevine.

In great trepidation, the vicar knocked at the door of Lizanben, which was opened by Elodie, currently an iceberg capable of sinking the poor vicar's impression of the *Titanic* with no trouble at all. Thinking very quickly indeed, she said, 'I'm so glad you asked me to come round' – ordered, more like – 'because I was going to come round today anyway to ask you a favour about Sunday.'

'What about Sunday?' asked Elodie, still standing at the door, her tone icy enough to fell small birds.

'I was wondering if you could play the organ. I thought I'd heard that you'd had some lessons, but I didn't know whether you would feel comfortable with doing it in front of the whole congregation.'

'Oh, come on in, do, Vicar. Whatever am I doing, keeping you out on the doorstep like this, as if you were a common tradesman? I'll just put on the kettle, then we can discuss this further.'

Good grief! The iceberg had melted into what were quite tropical waters. She had certainly thawed at the mention of playing the organ, and it surely seemed that she had, somehow, found out about Willard playing it and Thea taking the choir at their practice.

'We have no one else to rely on now,' she pleaded, her fingers crossed behind her back to negate the false sincerity she was oozing. 'In fact, I wonder if, when Willard gets back from France, you couldn't take over running the choir and, if possible, stand in for him, as well, on the organ? I haven't met anyone else in the congregation with such a knowledge of music.' – not yet, she thought, but I will, eventually, no matter how far I have to look and how much I have to try.

'I'll just bring the tray through. The tea must be brewed by now, but I'd be delighted. Perhaps we could get down to discussing music to be played during communion, and before and after the service.' There was always organ music whenever the congregation arrived and settled for the start of service and afterwards, when they were returning their hymn books and deciding whether to stay for a hot drink and a natter or to go straight home.

When she came in bearing a tray with all the accoutrements of refreshment, to be served in the finest of bone china, Rev. Florrie's heart sank, and she knew it would be some time before she would be able to get away.

'And we must plan the music for Albert's and poor Yvonne's funerals. Have you spoken to the relatives about any hymns they might like? I know the choir doesn't usually sing for funerals but, I think in these two events, they should, given whose funerals they are.'

'Marjorie Mundy let me have Mr Burton's son's telephone number, so I've been able to speak to him, and I've arranged to visit Mr Pooley later today.'

'Right you are. I need a list of the hymns for Sunday right now, if I'm to practise, and a key to the door, so that I can let myself in and lock up afterwards; hymns for the funeral, and any incidental music for them, as soon as possible, and hymns for next week …'

'I'm only asking you to cover this weekend. We don't know when the police will release Albert and Yvonne's bodies for burial. And the Scardifields will be back by the following Sunday. I just happen, however, to have the hymn list for choir practice and Sunday on me.'

'Thank you very much, Vicar,' intoned Miss Sutherland in a much colder voice, holding her hand out for the crumpled scrap of paper Florrie had pulled from her pocket, and taking it as if it were radioactive. 'And a spare key, if you'd be so kind?'

Rev. Florrie scrambled around in her over-full pockets and managed to produce the emergency church keys, scattering boiled sweets and tissues as she did so. 'I'll leave you to gather together your possessions and see yourself out, if you don't mind, I think I can hear Mummy calling me from upstairs.' Elodie Sutherland left the room, closing the door with a finality that indicated the audience was at a blessed and unexpected end. Florrie scrabbled about on the floor picking up the detritus that had escaped from her pockets and left the house with a sigh of relief.

Her next call was to Wheel Cottage to speak to David, Yvonne's widower. The house looked at her with blank eyes, and not a sound came from inside, although she had not expected a great deal of noise. David answered the door, his face still a mask of grief and disbelief. He must have taken compassionate leave.

'Come on in,' he said. 'The children have gone to their grandparents' for a while. I need the time to come to terms with this without dealing with their grief as well.'

'Thank you, Mr Pooley. I just wanted to discuss some of Yvonne's favourite hymns; it doesn't matter if they aren't funereal. I want to try to capture some of her love for music as we say our final goodbyes to her.'

'Would you like something to drink?'

'No thank you. I've just had a cup of very refined tea at the Sutherlands'.' Her attempt at a whimsical turn of phrase left him cold, and he replied to her earlier question with, 'How about "Fight the Good Fight" for a start?'

'Sorry? Is there something you'd like to tell me – in complete confidence, of course?'

'No. Honestly. Well, just that we weren't getting on very well at the moment. Our marriage wasn't that sunny.'

'If you ever need someone to talk to, not necessarily about something confidential, you know my door is always open to you. You are one of my flock, and I wouldn't like to think of you sitting suffering in silence.'

'That's very kind of you, Vicar.'

'Do call me Florrie.'

'And I'm David. To get back to hymns, she was always very fond of "The Day Thou Gavest Lord is Ended" and the one that goes with the tune "Finlandia", although I can't recollect the first line. Where's old Albert when you need him, eh?'

'If I can't find it, I wouldn't mind betting it's in one of his fabulous modern hymn books. He had a set of three of them in his house, you know.'

'"Be still my soul". That's how it starts. I've just remembered. That should help you a little bit. Apart from those two, I don't really mind what you do. Nothing will make her less dead, will it?'

'No, David. Only time and faith will lead us to comfort. Don't forget what I said about being there if you need someone to talk to.'

'I won't, Florrie.'

As she left, Falconer and Carmichael were just walking up the front garden path. 'Hello, you two,' she called. 'Be gentle with Mr Pooley. He's been through a lot lately.'

As had he, Falconer, but he had no intention of telling Mr Pooley all about his first run in with Baldy Davey first thing this morning! He had been sitting at his desk, as usual, when Carmichael made his entrance, the shock probably taking six months off the inspector's life-expectancy.

'What in the name of God have you done now, Carmichael? Yesterday was bad enough, but this is even worse,' he said in a horrified and slightly raised voice.

'Well, you know I said I had three choices, sir? Carmichael didn't even bother to sound apologetic at the shock he had just given his boss. 'I talked it over with Kerry, and we both agreed that this was the best choice. I have got a baseball cap in my pocket, if you'd prefer.'

The man's head had no trace of hair. It was shaved as bald as a billiard ball, and a radical change like that can drastically alter the way you see someone.

'Carmichael, you look more like someone that we're looking for: one of the thieves rather than a thief-taker. How are people going to open up to you when you look like a wrestler or an out-and-out thug?'

'I didn't think it looked that bad.'

'Then you need your eyes tested.'

'It'll soon grow back, and I bought some blackcurrant lollipops on the way here, so that I could do a Kojak.

'I shouldn't think anyone who doesn't devour old repeats of ancient American cop shows will even understand what a Kojak is, even if you explain it to them. And if you say, "Who loves ya, baby?"' just once, I shall ram any lollipops I can find about your person somewhere the sun definitely don't shine. Got it?'

'Got it, sir. So I can definitely wear the baseball hat?'

'I suppose so, or everyone'll wonder where I got the heavy from.'

'And *you* remembered who I was alluding to, didn't you? Are you watching it again?'

'No I am not, Sergeant.'

'You will treat him gently, won't you, sir?' muttered Carmichael.

Of course he'd go easy with the widower, if he didn't look in the least like a suspect. Falconer nodded, as if he didn't know how to do that. This was what a lot of his work was like; dealing with people who had received bad news of one sort or another. 'Hello, Mr Pooley,' the inspector greeted the householder holding out his warrant card. Carmichael followed suit, and Falconer continued, 'We'd just like another word with you, if that's all right?'

'Fine by me,' replied the newly widowed man, in a monotone. 'Got nothing else to do. He gave a quick wave to the vicar, Carmichael following suit with a much more flamboyant one, and the three of them went through to sit in the conservatory.

With the sunlight through the glass, it was very warm in there, and David asked Carmichael if he didn't want to take off his hat. 'No thank you, sir. I'm perfectly comfortable.' He was lying, but didn't want to get into any more trouble than he already had. Thank God he wasn't married to Falconer. Thank God no one else was either, he thought, as beads of sweat began to gather on his forehead and upper lip.

'I suppose this visit is about Yvonne's killer?' Mr Pooley asked, trying to remove any trace of emotion from his voice.

'It is,' replied Falconer, as Carmichael began to drip sweat on to his notebook. Thank goodness he wrote in pencil. 'But about a particular aspect of her life. We know how she died, but I would like to look into her relationship with Landbank Ltd.'

'As far as I know, she didn't have one.'

'Does the name Sheridan Grimble mean anything to you?'

'No,' replied Mr Pooley, wondering why there were snorts of muffled laughter, as Carmichael stuffed his handkerchief in his mouth. He had remembered the man's nose, glasses, and moustache, looking for all the world like a joke-shop disguise.

'What about Cardew Trevelyan?'

'No, nothing.' Pooley's face remained devoid of emotion as the sergeant finally managed to gain control of himself.

'Sigmund Aylesford?'

'No. Why are you asking me about all these men, inspector?'

'All in good time, Mr Pooley. Xavier Smallwood?'

The thunderclouds rolled in across David's forehead, and he snarled, although his reply was the same. 'No,' he denied, but it was more clipped this time.

'Are you absolutely certain about that last one?'

'Yes! Who the hell are they all, anyway?' he almost yelled, his colour high.

'Calm down, Mr Pooley. They are the only four employees of Landbank Ltd. Do you think it likely that your wife knew any of them?'

'NO!' he roared. 'She didn't know anybody from that bloody company.'

Leaving the subject for now, Falconer cleared his throat and said, as calmly as he could, 'I'm afraid we shall have to take away her computer.'

'Why? No! You can't take it.' Pooley was up, now, ready for conflict.

'Carmichael,' said Falconer, confidently, and the big sergeant rose to his feet and stood in front of Mr Pooley, while Falconer walked into the sitting room to see two computers in front of him, one open and one closed.

The one that was being used was opened on an undertaker's site, no doubt comparing prices. Even death need not be too expensive these days, which was crucial if you had a mortgage and two children. They had already checked, and there was no life insurance on the organist.

Picking up the 'sleeping' laptop, he went out of the door, calling Carmichael after him, as if he were calling a dog – which he well might have been – a large one, guarding his master's safety.

On their way back to the police station to hand over the computer to the technical geeks, Falconer said, 'He was quite a big man himself. What made him calm down and let me take the laptop in the end?'

'I took my hat off, sir, and sort of gurned at him.'

'That would work for anyone, Carmichael. I don't know why the army doesn't use you for scaring off the enemy.'

'*Sir*!

'Sorry, I didn't mean to insult you. It's just that you do look just a little bit scary with your head shaved – and with you gurning at him, well, I'd have backed off, too, in his position.'

At the counter of the canteen, the woman who usually made sure 'her Davey' was looked after, looked up from giving the food containers a stir and screamed. The cook came out of the kitchen, and she yelled too. They ended up holding on to each other for protection and just carried on roaring.

Holding up a hand to them, Falconer shouted above the noise, 'It's only DS Carmichael. He's had a little accident with his hair.'

The serving woman was the first to recover, and she said emphatically, 'A little accident? That's what he'd had yesterday. He must have had quite a big accident, because there's not a follicle to be seen now. Who did this to yer, Davey love? You tell me and I'll give them a good going over. So will you, won't you?' she asked, turning to the cook, who nodded in agreement.

'Calm down, ladies, and I'm sure the DC will explain.' They waited with their arms folded. This had better be good. Davey Carmichael was their favourite, and whoever was responsible would have them to answer to.

'It's all my fault, ladies. You saw yesterday that I'd had

a bit of bother with the colour?' said Carmichael, realising that this explanation was one he would probably have to do again and again.

'Well, I talked it over with my wife, and we decided that there were three options for me. I could either tough it out, which I didn't feel up to; I could wait for it to grow a bit, and have blonde tips, which I think have gone out of fashion now, or I could get rid of it. We had a chat last night and I got her to help me shave it off. It'll grow quick enough, and I have got a baseball cap with me for when the lads come in.'

Too late! 'Ooh, is that a bowling ball I see before me?' called the voice of PC Merv Green.

'No, I reckon that's a football,' replied DC Roberts, who had missed the sight this morning, having arrived late – again – and been distracted.

'You leave him alone,' yelled a voice from behind the counter. It was the cook's, and the serving lady was actually coming round from behind the counter to give them a good telling off.

'If you pick on this poor lad after what he's been through, I'll get to hear about it and I'll serve none of you, ever again. And I'll make your lives hell for bullying. Do you want to go hungry or thirsty? If not, you'd better think on. You'll have us both to answer to, and we hear everything that goes on in this station.'

That shut them up, but Falconer and Carmichael still decided to take their coffee and Danishes back to the office.

'And you can pass that on to all the others, especially that Bob Bryant down there on the desk. I'll not be wanting to hear of this lad being jeered at every time he comes in or goes out of the station.' The voice of the serving woman followed them all the way down the corridor.

'That sounds like you sorted, until you're less follically

challenged, Carmichael,' said Falconer grinning up at his sergeant.

'They might not use words, but they'll find some other way of getting at me,' the sergeant replied.

'Then go and tell … what are their names?'

'Josie's the server and Vi's the cook, sir.'

'Let them know, and they'll be after whoever's extracting the Michael like the hounds of hell, and they'll never eat in this canteen again.'

'Very wild west.'

'In our case, very wild *south* west.'

When Rev. Florrie turned up for choir practice, a very sorry sight met her eyes. There had been a whole row of children before, and now there was only a straggle of women in the left-hand stalls. 'Where are all the children?' she asked, nonplussed. She had had no phone calls of apology.

'Their parents got together and decided they didn't feel safe leaving their little ones in a place where there had been two recent murders. I got a phone call about two hour ago,' explained Elodie Sutherland, rather smugly, in Florrie's opinion.

'Well, why didn't you phone me and tell me?'

'It wouldn't have made any difference, and you'd find out soon enough,' came the superior answer. Bummer, thought Florrie, resigning herself to a very depleted choir until the culprit or culprits had been apprehended.

Ian Brown was the only one at all on the men's side, because Willard was sitting at the organ running through the hymns in his own inimitable fashion, as the vicar realised that Mr Scardifield wasn't the best sight-reader in the world; in fact, he probably wasn't the best sight-reader in the church at this very moment. But he could do the pedals, and no one else could, apart from the budding organist, bossy Elodie.

Trust her to have chosen a hymn with four sharps and one with four flats. There was a lesson to be learnt there. When Willard was playing, she would have to be a little less concerned with which hymns were appropriate to that particular Sunday, and give a little more thought to what keys the accompaniments were in. It didn't matter so much for the singers, because most of them were just reading the words, but Willard needed to be at least fifty per cent accurate for them to get through all the verses necessary.

Clapping her hands to attract attention, she looked around at her depleted troops with a sinking heart. This wouldn't do at all, unless those who were left could make a really angelic and, more importantly, loud noise, to lead the congregation.

'Right, we'll start, Willard, with number 517, "Ye Holy Angels Bright" which was my favourite hymn when I was a child. Everyone know it?' Heads nodded. 'Off you go Willard, ladies, heads up and smile.' At least this one was in C major, she was relieved to notice – no sharps or flats to trip up the unwary fingers or thumbs.

A lame mooing accompanied the awful accompaniment and, just for a moment, Rev. Florrie thought that maybe Victor Borge had snuck in and taken Willard's place at the organ. No such luck. At least Mr Borge could play when he wanted to.

Clapping her hands again, this time with a little less confidence, she suggested they had a go at 'O For a Thousand Tongues to Sing', but from a tune in a different book. That presented a problem – reading the words from one book and the music from another.

'Allow me to take over, as you did ask me to take the practice, Vicar,' came the dulcet tones of Elodie Sutherland, with just an edge of impatience.

'I'm so sorry, Miss Sutherland. Please, take over: I don't know what I'm doing. I'll sing with the sopranos, shall I?'

'Good idea, Vicar, and leave the musical direction to someone who knows what they're doing.'

'Smug bitch,' muttered Florrie from her place in the chancel, but nevertheless took a place in the ladies' stalls and opened her hymnal.

The tune was a tricky one from an accompanying point of view, and Willard floundered around as if looking for the lost chord. Eventually, Elodie stopped waving her hands around in a parody of a conductor, and suggested that they tried it unaccompanied. '*A capella*,' she informed them, with a smug expression. 'That means without the organ. Give us the opening chord, please, Willard, so that they can get their notes.' Didn't that make it sound grand?

The result was rather more like a musical fight than a hymn, with everyone singing a different tune or in a different key. After three or four attempts, Florrie said she'd look for something where the tune was better known. There'd been no trouble with this particular tune in her old parish, as it was one they had sung for years. Not so here in Ford Hollow. She'd have to run everything past both the organist and choir mistress if she was to survive, musically, without being branded a holy fool.

'309 if you don't mind, Miss Sutherland. "For the Beauty of the Earth". We had a bit of a mix-up last week. Willard, you take your communion first, then start to play while the choir takes its. After that, we go to the communion hymn, which is the one to accompany the adults coming to the altar rail, and the children to be blessed. Is that clear?'

Elodie Sutherland cleared her throat pointedly, glared at Florrie, and took over again. Oh God, this one's got two flats, thought the vicar. I hope Willard can cope. He did, after a fashion, but the vocals were thin and flat, and Miss Sutherland held up a hand to halt the singers. As most of them had their noses in their hymn books, however, this didn't have the desired effect.

'Stop, oh stop that dreadful noise. What's got into you all? Eyes up from your books, or the sound just goes down into your hymnal and is completely lost. Thea Scardifield, you are singing flat. I want you to pay a little more attention to tuning when you sing, if you don't mind.'

'I was not flat!' declared Thea, going bright red. 'I've spent my whole life in church choirs and choral societies, and I never sing flat.'

'I don't give a fig for what you've done in the past; you're singing flat today, and I want you to be careful of your tuning, or you'll put the others off.'

'How on earth can I put the others off, when they're all singing in different keys and at different rates?'

'They seemed perfectly all right to me,' Elodie was smiling openly, with the heady awareness of power.

'That's it. I won't even be here on Sunday, so you can stick your choir practice. I'm going home to pack.' Her husband, Willard, had his shoulders hunched at the organ, not wishing to get involved in a verbal tussle with either of the protagonists in this little production.

As Thea purposely shut the heavy oak door with as much force as she could manage, Elodie looked at Florrie and asked her if there was anything else she wanted them to run through, as she thought the anthem and seven-fold amen should be shelved for now.

'I wouldn't mind you having a go at number 289, "Come ye Thankful People, Come". It's very nearly time for our harvest festival, and I'd like this particular hymn to be really punchy.' Great! Only one flat this time. Willard must be able to manage it.

After the first verse, it was she that stopped the practice. 'That simply won't do,' she announced. 'The pace is like that of an arthritic tortoise, and listen to the words. Just listen to them. Raise the sound of harvest-home!' she sang, loudly and enthusiastically, then repeated it in a depressed and lugubrious voice, which raised a titter of laughter.

'Do it the way I sang it first. "*Raise* the sound of *harvest-home!*" There's an exclamation mark at the end of that line. Sing it. This is a hymn full of thanks for a harvest safely gathered in. Make it sound like a thanksgiving, not a dirge.'

'Thank you very much, Vicar,' snarled Elodie Sutherland, not at all grateful for the interruption. 'Right, we have a couple of weeks to work on that one and get it sufficiently jolly for the vicar. We'll just have to see how things go on Sunday.'

'Don't forget I'm going away tomorrow,' boomed the deep voice of Willard Scardifield from the organ.

'That's all right. I'll be playing,' replied Elodie, without batting an eyelash. 'The vicar's already given me the emergency key, so I'll have plenty of time to practise between now and Sunday.' God, how smug she was, thought Florrie, momentarily running low on Christian charity.

When she got home at seven thirty, she knew that something had to be done before Sunday, or it would hardly be worth having the service, especially as it was a sung Eucharist. Picking up the little black book that she had already started in this parish, she began to phone round the members of the Mothers' Union. Surely they would come to her aid in the case of an emergency?

She put her situation on the telephone to Marjorie Mundy, whom she knew would be unable to stand in the stalls, or sing, but she valued her opinion. 'Just put it on a bit, and you shouldn't have too much trouble,' she advised.

Rev. Florrie did put it on a bit. 'It doesn't matter if you can't sing. Do the notes you can and mime the rest. I just want the choir stalls to look full to give confidence to the rest of the congregation after what's happened since I've arrived.' That did sound bad, didn't it, as if everything were, somehow, her fault for turning up in the first place?

'Look, all I want to do is to put on a show of solidarity for those coming to the service. It doesn't have to be fantastic. It's more about numbers than anything else. Can you come tomorrow morning at ten o'clock for a quick run through?'

Eventually she had got hold of all the members of the MU and whined, begged, and pleaded until she had elicited their cooperation. Elodie Sutherland had also agreed to play the organ for this impromptu practice, and she felt she had done all she could to make the following Sunday a success after their two tragedies.

Chapter Thirteen

Saturday

Rev. Florrie unlocked the church door on Saturday morning, then went for a little walk through the churchyard, looking at some of the older gravestones. When she returned just before practice was due to start, she was absolutely delighted to see the women's stalls bursting at the seams, with a face she had never seen before in the front of the stalls opposite.

Elodie Sutherland was bustling round in her alb and collar, bearing them like a badge of office, but stopped to indicate the new face and introduce her as Anne Rittscher, eighteen years old, who was studying modern languages, and had just come back from an exchange visit in Germany. She represented the other fifty per cent of the alto section, but Elodie assured her that Anne had a strong voice and read music easily.

This looked more the ticket. Miss Sutherland then did something that Rev. Florrie would have thought impossible, if the idea had ever been put to her. She actually asked Florrie if she would be so good as to take the choir, because she would be fully occupied with playing the organ. 'I've been having lessons, you know, so I think I can manage the hymns.' She had really handed over the choir to someone else. Who would have thought it? Florrie thought she might put a baton in her hair and nod her head backwards and forward, in time with the beat.

The vicar pulled herself together and addressed the suddenly full choir stalls.

'We just want to give the service a bit of oomph. You never know, some of you might enjoy it, and you could join as a regular singer. If you can't reach a note because it's too high or too low, don't go for it and get it out of tune. Just mime. I'm sure you're going to be absolutely fabulous.' Her fingers were crossed behind her back for good luck again.

They certainly were better than the shower that had sung the night before. There was power in numbers, and they made a fair fist of everything, with Anne and her oppo powering out the alto part so that it could be heard, booming across from what had before been the side inhabited only by the paltry number of men.

Although Willard was away, and Albert was dead, Ian Brown sang as loudly as he could, but it was the overall volume that was important for now. Revitalising the choir and trying to find new members was something Florrie could work on when she had settled in a bit better, and got to know more people.

Suddenly the vicar felt happy that things were going to go well for her in this new parish, despite what had happened recently, and she was grinning broadly as the rehearsal came to an end. Thanking everyone sincerely, she said she would see them in the morning and looked forward to the sound they would make from the front of the church.

The newly rounded up choristers began to leave the church, chattering like a group of starlings, until only Florrie and Elodie Sutherland were left. Failing to slip away unnoticed, Florrie noticed with apprehension that the older woman was approaching her with a beatific smile on her face. 'What can I do for you, Miss Sutherland?' she asked, only to have the woman reply with, 'Oh, please call me Elodie. I should like that so much.'

'OK, Elodie, what can I do for you?'

'I wondered if you could hear my confession? I haven't had it heard for so long that I sometimes feel weighted down with un-absolved sin.'

'But surely, we have the general confession in the Eucharist service. Does that not absolve you?'

'Not really. It just seems to skip over everything, and I feel a personal confession cleanses the soul so much more. Of course, if you don't want to do it, I could go to Rev. Monaghan, but he does tend to be a bit scathing about it.'

'Of course I'll hear your confession. You don't want to be going anywhere near that man if you can help it.'

'Well done you, Vicar, for the other evening. You did what a lot of we ladies have wanted to do for years.'

Surprised at this approval, Florrie replied, 'It really hurt my hand, though.'

'He won't get away with things the way he used to. Now, where can we go for this confession? Going back a while, the old vicar used to do it in his vestry.'

'Suits me, er, Elodie. I'll just robe up and we'll go in there, so that I can lock up to ensure our privacy.'

There were, indeed, two chairs in the vestry, but as Elodie Sutherland began her confession, 'Forgive me Fath ... What do I call you? OK. Forgive me, Vicar, for I have sinned ...' Elodie elucidated all the usual trivial things that take up so much confession time for Catholic priests, but then things suddenly got more serious.

'And I need to tell you that I was responsible for the deaths of Albert Burton and Yvonne Pooley.' Here she stopped and looked Rev. Florrie in the eye. There was no confessional box here, with a wooden lattice in between confessor and sinner to protect identity.

'You are?'

'Yes. Now you can see why I need confession. Their deaths were my fault.'

Florrie's head was spinning. Here she was, locked in

the vestry with a double murderer, and there was no way out that wouldn't reveal her panic. What should she do?

'And what did you do to bring about these deaths?' was the only question she could think of; which was just as well.

'I had such evil thoughts about them that I willed them to die,' replied the repressed spinster.

'You willed them …'

'I wanted them to die. It was me.'

'Miss Sutherland, I can absolve you for the sins of having wicked thought, but that doesn't mean that they died because of what you thought.'

'It doesn't?'

'Of course not. Now, go and do some Hail Marys or whatever it is you do for penance – I don't know. You're absolved of all the other bits and pieces, and of your evil thoughts. Now, be off with you.'

'That doesn't seem very professional. I hadn't finished,' squeaked Elodie.

'And I don't feel very professional at the moment. Now, stop wasting my time with silly fantasies. You can't will someone dead, neither can you kill them by thought power. I would have thought you were intelligent enough to know that.'

'But I hadn't finished … Very well, I must be off. Mummy will need me.' Elodie waited while Florrie unlocked the door, then positively swished out of the vestry and the church.

In Market Darley, both Falconer and Carmichael were on duty that weekend, having only been on call the last one, and would have the next one free. Carmichael had arrived very glum-faced, his baseball cap on back to front, now that no one ever wore it that way any more.

'Who pissed in your cornflakes?' asked Falconer.

Carmichael smiled at this question form, and admitted

that it was Merv Green who had upset him. 'He must've snuck up on my car when I was getting out of it, and as I locked the doors' – this could take ages, as Carmichael still had not fixed his Russian roulette central locking – 'he knocked off my baseball cap, and said, 'Hello, Baldilocks. Give us a kiss then.' I said I'd set Josie from the canteen on him, as she thought of me as one of her sons, and he said he didn't care, because she thought of him as her fantasy lover. No contest.'

'I'll have a word with him, and you tell Josie, see what she makes of her paramour, now that he's been revealed in his true colours. He'd better not want porridge for breakfast, for there'll be no oats for him for a while.'

'Very funny, sir. Perhaps I'll tell PC Starr' – PC Green's fiancée – 'and she'll tell him to leave me alone.'

'Of course,' added Falconer, in light-hearted mood, 'perhaps you could get your head henna-tattooed. That's only temporary, and it would at least cover your baldness while the hair grew back.'

'Brilliant idea, sir. I'll see about it in my lunch break.'

'I wasn't serious, Sergeant. Please don't go out and do it. It'll only make things even worse.'

'But ...' Carmichael had that stubborn look on his face that Falconer was getting to know so well.

'No, Carmichael. I absolutely forbid it. I'll phone Kerry and ask her what she thinks,' threatened the inspector, then thought better of it. With that pair, the whole thing could backfire in his face.

Falconer's attention was suddenly caught by something in his e-mail, and he found a message from the technical boys stating that there were two types of anonymous e-mails on Yvonne Pooley's computer, copies attached.

There were, indeed, two completely different sorts: threatening and seductive. One set told her to lay off Landbank Ltd or it would be the worse for her, and did she really want to see her children grow up, or for them to die young? The other was about her physical attractions and what the sender would like to do to her.

'Come and look at this, Carmichael,' he called over to the younger man's desk.

'Woo-hoo,' replied Carmichael. 'Who are they from?'

'They both look like they were sent from blind e-mail addresses, but they were both sent, it would appear, from Landbank Ltd. There are a couple of people we will want to be talking to again. And no wonder Mr Pooley got so hot under the collar when we mentioned the company. He'd obviously been having a little spy on his wife's machine too. It could even have been he who was out for his wife's blood.'

'But it doesn't answer the question about who killed Albert Burton.' No matter how uncomfortable this made Falconer feel, Carmichael had got right to the heart of the matter.

'She could have come back to the church with her husband in tow, in the middle of an almighty row, and Albert just happened to be there. Maybe Mr Pooley killed him just to shut him up. Maybe he just wanted to stop him interrupting, and the man was frailer than he thought.'

'It's a possibility, sir. But how would he stop his wife from going to the police? Why should she keep her mouth shut? And what about the threatening emails from Landbank?'

'One of them went to meet her there, and Albert just got in the way? Same scenario, really.' Falconer was just about fresh out of ideas. Albert was always the fly in the ointment whenever he hit on a possible scenario. The two murders didn't seem to have anything in common: an elderly man whose only interest was church music, and a married woman with two children who just happened to run the choir and play the organ. They had very little in common.

'OK, sir, we'll go with what we've got for now. Who

are we talking about from the land company?'

'The architect, Sheridan Grimble, for the anonymous threats, and the surveyor, Xavier Smallwood, for the anonymous endearments. They may have set up e-mail accounts that didn't reveal their names, but they forgot the most basic of precautions; getting the recipient to delete the messages from their system, and even then, the technical boys would have been able to recover them. It's as bad as committing yourself to writing love letters – worse really, because you can at least recover letters and burn them, and they're gone.'

'So that's three we want to bring in for questioning: Pooley, Grimble, and Smallwood? Do you want to do it now, sir?

'I think they'll keep until Monday when we've got a fuller staff. I can't see any of them suspecting that they've been rumbled, and fleeing the country. Can you?'

'Who had Roberts set up for us with the planners?'

'Good point, Carmichael. He's got us an appointment with the chief planning officer for Monday morning, and with a couple of councillors from the planning committee for the afternoon. I want to go over to Ford Hollow again and speak to Rev. Florrie to see if anything else has come to mind, or whether she's been privy to any more gossip or confidences.'

'In that case, would you like to come and meet my uncle, sir?' Falconer's face clouded as he remembered a previous visit to one of the sergeant's uncles, where he had a view of the dog-breeding set up that was much too close for comfort. With Carmichael involved, it ended in mud. How else could it have ended?

Seeing his face, Carmichael immediately added, 'It's not the uncle we went to before. It's one on the other side of the family, and his new bitch had a litter not long ago. I thought it would be good to see the pups. And I promise it won't be muddy at this time of year. Please, sir. I haven't seen them yet.'

'Go on, then,' agreed the inspector. What harm could it do, to look at a few puppies? 'Are you going to the canteen for lunch first?'

'No way, sir. I'm going out for lunch, and I'm going now. I'll be back for us to visit my uncle on the way to, or the way back from Ford Hollow; whichever you prefer. Shall we take my car?'

'No way, José. Now, get yourself off. Not after last time.'

The inspector heard the office door open and turned round to smile at his colleague, but his jaw dropped before he could utter a greeting. 'You did it?' he squeaked. 'You did it, after all I said?'

'It's a bit nifty, isn't it, sir?' asked Carmichael, running a hand over his newly henna-tattooed head.

'Whatever will Kerry say about it?'

'I phoned her on my mobile and, as I told her it was only temporarily until my hair grows back, she said to go ahead. She thought it would be a hoot.'

'Twit-twoo,' sighed Falconer. Before he could stand up to leave, his phone rang, and he found Bob Bryant on the end, informing him that the station had just received an anonymous call to say that Rev. Monaghan had been seen in Ford Hollow around the time of the first murder. 'We'll add him to our list for Monday, Bob. Thanks a bunch for that.'

Florrie greeted the two detectives enthusiastically, and led them to sit round the kitchen table. 'I've got all the goss from the line dancing for you, and all the chaos with the choir, as well as having a parishioner confess to the murders,' she said, and watched their faces as this information sank in.

'What? Who? When?' this was Falconer.

'Crikey!' Carmichael was a man of fewer words.

'Well, would you credit it, Carmichael?' asked Falconer on their way to the sergeant's uncle's newly established dog-breeding business. 'I say, that looks a bit more salubrious than the last place you took me.'

Before them stood a venerable farmhouse, in reasonable order, and not a wreck, like the one they had been to before. 'Why is the gate locked with that huge padlock?'

'Because the pups and their parents are very valuable, and he needs to keep out burglars. The house and kennels are alarmed as well.'

'That sounds a little more professional. What do we do to attract his attention?'

'I ring him on my mobile, and tell him we're waiting to be let in.'

'He is security conscious, isn't he?'

Carmichael made his call, and a man of about fifty came round from the back of the house, dressed in tired old tweeds, to let them in. 'Hello there, Davey boy. Who's your friend?'

'This is my boss, Detective Inspector Falconer,' replied Carmichael.

'Call me Harry. And you are?'

'Dennis,' replied the stout figure, holding out a polite hand through the gate. 'I'll just let you in, then we'll go round the back and I'll introduce you to the pups. Little darlings, they are. You'll love them.'

'I'll decide how I feel about them.' Falconer was not ready to commit himself.

Uncle Dennis led them round to the rear of the house where there was a huge enclosure, and let them in. 'I expect they're all having a nap at the moment,' he said, then smiled at what seemed to be a small hairy horse cantering out of what, to him, resembled a stable block, and increasing its pace as it saw that there were visitors.

'Come on, baby,' called Carmichael as the thing approached, reached out and stroked its head. Come on, let's play.' He actually got down on the ground which was, fortunately dry, and began to tickle the animal's tummy and nuzzle its fur, making cooing noises that would have embarrassed a nursery nurse.

'I thought you said your uncle bred dogs, not horses,' said Falconer nervously backing away. 'Is this one running in the four-thirty today?'

'This is just one of the puppies, sir.'

'Puppies of what? The Hound of the Baskervilles? And how big are the parents?'

Both of his questions were answered simultaneously, as Carmichael informed him that his uncle bred Irish wolfhounds. And then Mummy strolled out of the stable-like building to sniff the air.

'Look at that bloody great monster!' croaked the inspector, as Mummy began to move towards them in a leisurely but curious way. 'Hide me! She'll eat me.'

'Don't be so silly, sir. She's just coming to see where her pup has gone.'

Mummy, scenting a friend in Carmichael, who had visited her before she whelped, came thundering over, screeching to a halt just in front of the two men. Then another scent assailed her nostrils, and it was good. She turned to Falconer and began to whine piteously as she sniffed where the legs of his trousers joined. She had to lean her head down to do this, he was terrified to notice.

'Don't sniff there. It's embarrassing,' squeaked Falconer, trying to cover his sensitive bits with his hands. This huge beast would make only a light snack out of his meat and two veg, and he needed them. He would, eventually, like a family, and didn't want his chances of this happening cut off in such a bizarre fashion.

'She's just being friendly, sir.'

'It doesn't feel friendly.'

'Pat her head. She's only looking for attention,' Carmichael reassured him, but the inspector could see the attention the dog would get – from the press. He could see tomorrow's headlines: 'DI mauled to death by giant dog'. He began to back away, the hairs on the back of his neck standing on end with fear. 'DI loses family jewels in dog attack'.

'Stand your ground, sir. She's really very friendly.'

The only thing that Falconer could stand now, was getting as far away from this enormous creature as quickly as possible. He turned and started to run towards the outer perimeter at the end of the long garden.

'Don't run, sir. She'll think you're playing,' called Carmichael in warning,' but it was no good, and the dog set off after him, just loping, not in hot pursuit. Mummy wanted to prolong the game for as long as possible with this man who smelled so interesting.

'Stop, sir. Let her know you're not going to play with her.'

'It's her playing with me that I'm worried about,' puffed Falconer over his shoulder. At the very end of the garden there was just a short fence and when he saw the dog on his tail, he speeded up as much as possible, certain that he could jump the fence.

He couldn't, and it was no ordinary fence, but an electrified one topped with barbed wire. 'Help!' the helpless man called, now caught like a fly in a spider's web, just waiting to be devoured.

'Stay still or you'll only get more tangled.'

'Get this creature off me. For God's sake will somebody help me?' He was now getting indignant, as well as furious and terrified, all at the same time.

Carmichael and Uncle Dennis rushed to his aid, Dennis calling Mummy away, telling her to 'sit' and 'stay'.

'Look at my trousers, Carmichael. They're ruined.'

'It's your own fault, if you don't mind me saying so,' said Uncle Dennis in a miffed voice. 'If you'd stopped when you were told to, this wouldn't have happened. She's the gentlest of dogs, and just thought you wanted a romp.'

'If I'd wanted a romp, I wouldn't have chosen this racehorse-lookalike to have had it with.'

'You *were* told not to run.'

'Get me off this blasted wire and, while you're at it, turn off the current. If I move even slightly, I come into contact with it again, and it's near a very sensitive area.'

'I'll do that, and get the wire clippers while I'm at it, but look what you've done to my blasted deterrent. It'll be ruined by the time I've cut you free, and I'll have to spend the rest of the afternoon redoing it.'

'I'll try not to bleed on the grass,' snarled Falconer sarcastically.

'You do that, and it'll be attracting all the animals from miles around. I don't want my precious stock unsettled.'

Falconer, speechless as he was, noticed that Carmichael had his handkerchief stuffed in his mouth to stop him laughing out loud.

Regaining the power of speech, he hissed, 'You just wait until I get you back to the station. I'm going to make you take your baseball hat off and go to the canteen. I bet Josie's no match for a bunch of lads who are just coming off duty or on their break, even with Vi at her side.'

'You wouldn't, sir?'

'The amount these trousers cost me, I damned well would.'

'What if I said no?'

'It would be an order, not a request.'

'Oh, help!' Carmichael looked devastated at this threat.

As Uncle Dennis approached holding a formidable pair of wire cutters, he called, 'Why have you got a hat on in this gorgeous weather, Davey lad? Sure it's a lovely warm day. Take it off, son, take it off.'

Being naturally obedient to his elders, especially those who were also family, Carmichael did so, giving his uncle the best laugh he'd had in months. 'What a card you are, to be sure. Why on earth did you have that done to you?'

'It's a long story, Uncle Dennis. I'll tell you when we've got more time.'

'Look at the mess you've made of me good weeds,' stated Uncle Dennis, but his humour had improved, and the corners of his mouth were twitching, probably from the good laugh he had had at his nephew. 'You've bled all over them. Take your hat off again, Davey.'

Davey obliged, and Uncle Dennis laughed so hard that he leant down and held on to his knees, bent double.

'Ahem,' coughed Falconer. If you don't mind, I'm in pain here.'

'Right you are, sir. Then we'll get you up to the house and I'll let you wash your wounds and provide you with some sticking plasters.'

Do we have to go past those damned great dogs again?'

'We do, that.'

Falconer stood motionless for a few moments, weighing up his choices. Run the gauntlet of the dogs again, or bleed on the seats of the Boxster? 'You can go one either side of me and protect me, while you get me to the house.' He had made his decision, and just hoped he didn't live to regret it.

Driving home, his hands a disaster area of plasters on the steering wheel, Carmichael asked, 'Would you like to drop in at mine and borrow that pair of jogging bottoms again? You trousers are rather ripped.'

'You are kidding, aren't you? And meet Mulligan again, and have him smell a strange dog on me? Not on your life.'

'You're right. He'd be broken-hearted.'

'That's not exactly what I mean, Sergeant. No, I'm going to drop you off at the station, then I'm going home for the day. Any emergencies, ring me. I'm not going back to the station unless I have to. I'll write up my notes at home.'

'Yes, sir.' Carmichael felt thoroughly chastened again, but at least he wouldn't be forced into the canteen without his baseball cap, which he secretly enjoyed wearing back to front now that no one else did.

When he had got home, showered, and put on some un-shredded clothing, Falconer sat down to make some notes. On Monday they had an appointment with Michael Greenslade, the chief planning officer, and they had two interviews to conduct with councillors in the afternoon. They also had to pick up Pooley, Smallwood, Grimble, and Rev. Monaghan for questioning, and he wanted to go back over some of the other witness statements again, and question them further. There was a long way to go before they solved his one – these two!

Having put everything into his electronic diary, he grabbed the book he was currently reading and settled down on the settee, smiling as he slowly grew a furry blanket of cats. How much gentler and more civilised they were than dogs, he thought, forgetting about the bit where they tortured spiders or tore small animals and birds to shreds.

They were also so much more independent. They could let themselves in and out through the cat-flap, were self-cleaning, like his cooker, and they exercised themselves. Taken all round, they were the perfect pet for someone who worked, and excellent company, especially in the cool or cold weather.

Considering the weather, he thought the fairly fine spell they had been enjoying, with the exception of the occasion on which he and Carmichael had got soaked to the skin, seemed like it might be coming to an end. The bright daylight suddenly disappeared as dark clouds obscured what was left of the sun for today, and he had to move a few sleeping felines to turn on the light.

Taking a quick peek out of the window, he could discern storm clouds gathering on the horizon to join their paler counterparts over Market Darley and, no doubt, there would be rain before long. Stretching out on the settee once more, he found that there were more warm bodies creeping on to his supine form. Even the cats were aware that the temperature had dropped. Their little spot of Indian summer seemed as if it were over.

With any luck, he thought, a bit of bad weather would keep the criminals indoors, and he could catch up with some of the necessary paperwork and reports that went with this job. To the sound of multiple purrs, he dozed off, happy and content with his lot.

Chapter Fourteen

Sunday

In the vicarage at Ford Hollow, Rev. Florrie was up before seven o'clock, as she had to be in the church before seven-thirty for early communion. Possibly no one would come, but it gave her a chance to take her own, as she could not break her fast until afterwards. Then she would not have to be back there until just before the ten o'clock Eucharist. Today was also a family service, so she hoped that there would be more parents there with their children who didn't normally come just for a sung Eucharist, and whose children did not attend Sunday school.

Silas Slater also rose at the same hour, as he particularly wanted to take early communion this morning, so that he could assure the new vicar that he would sort out trimming and renewing, where necessary, the candles. She needn't come in earlier than she had to just to do that, as he'd taken it upon himself to carry out this task years ago, but he didn't know whether she'd remember from last week, as so much had happened since her arrival. He also liked to ensure that the sanctuary light was still burning, and check a few other minor details before he prepared his thurible and robed up.

'You off to the early one, then, this Sunday?' asked his wife from under the bedclothes, in a voice husky from sleep.

'Just this once, to make sure we both know our routines,' he replied, pulling his still-buttoned shirt from the day before over his head. He wouldn't put on clean clothes until after he'd showered.

'Well, don't you go making a habit of it. I like my lie-in of a Sunday, and I'm properly woken up now. Might as well get up and have my breakfast.'

'You loll about there for a while, and I'll come back and we can have it together.'

'I'll use the shower while you're gone. That way I can take as long as I like, and we'll eat together when you get back.' Sylvia Slater wasn't so bothered about eating before communion. She reckoned it was a bit daft, and far too Roman for her, not to eat as soon as she got up.

She drowsed, thinking about this, then cursing the head of the team ministry. St Cuthbert's had been what she thought of as an ordinary church until Rev. Monaghan had been appointed, introducing those horrible Alternative Service Books, and all the bells and smells of High Church.

She did not approve of what she called Anglo-Catholic rituals, and now you couldn't move for people bowing when they stood in the aisle facing the altar, or genuflecting at the slightest provocation. She'd preferred the simple services of old, when they said the service instead of sung it, and anyone could come in and join them without having to know the tunes to the sung bits.

Turning over with a smile, she remembered the other night, when Rev. Florrie had lumped that stinky old vicar one and told him to keep his hands to himself. That was really good. Then she remembered that she wanted a nice, long shower, and hauled herself out from under the covers. If she didn't get a move on, Silas would be back, and singing all the hymns they would be singing later as the water poured over him.

And, good golly, she was in the choir today, wasn't she? She really would have to get her skates on, if she was to get there in time to slip into the choir vestry and get into her alb, so she was fit to process down the aisle. Oh, how she now wished she'd asked if they could practise the procession yesterday morning. Silas had told her that it wasn't as easy as it looked, and she'd be holding a hymn book.

When he had returned and showered, while Sylvia fried bacon, eggs, and tomatoes, she asked him about processing, but he assured her it was easy, as long as you kept to a steady pace, and resisted the urge to run. After they had eaten, he took himself off to the church to sort out all his jobs, calling out, 'Good luck in the choir. We'll walk back together after the service, as you'll have to get out of your robe as well.' Silas wore a cream-coloured chasuble, marking him out from all the others involved in the service, with the exception of the vicar.

'Are we not staying for a cuppa?'

'Not today. I want to look at some wallpaper samples for the spare bedroom.'

He unlocked the door of the church and let himself in just as the rain began to pelt down. Pushing it slightly to, to keep the water out, he sorted out the candles, checked the sanctuary light, and checked also that the hymn and service books were all tidy, then he repaired to the vestry – the one at the front of the church just off the chancel, not the one at the rear, which was for the choir. Now it was time to prepare his thurible for the service, which took about half an hour.

He went to the area of wooden shelf that he usually used for this, opened his thurible, and put it down, removing the boat for the incense from the little cupboard where he also kept his tongs.

A figure slipped unnoticed into the church, removing a rain-bespattered mackintosh and hanging it on a hook in the choir vestry so that it wouldn't be seen. The person then crouched down, hiding between two pews, using a couple of hassocks for a cushion. Outside thunder began to roll and crash, and flashes of lightning suddenly lit up the church, exposing the position of the hidden figure.

It left its first hiding place, and took up a second position behind the ladies' choir stall, completely hidden from the vicar's vestry. Everything that was necessary to be known could be discerned by sound. There was no need to have a good view of what was going on. The figure actually closed its eyes now, concentrating as hard as possible on its sense of hearing.

Back in the vestry, Silas slipped his robe over his head and tied it at the waist, then took up a piece of charcoal with his tongs and started to attempt to light it. When it was finally alight, he dropped it into the copper dish in the thurible, and poked at it and blew, until it was able to retain the burning coal to its place. He then closed the thurible and prepared to 'set' his piece of charcoal.

He ought, at this point, to have taken it outside and swung it round vertically to assist the glowing, but he only went as far as the church porch today. This was no weather to be going right out into the open. Giving it a good swing, so that the precious piece of fire should not extinguish itself, he then returned inside and hung it from a nail in a beam outside the vestry door.

Everything he had done was identifiable by sound to the one who waited, hidden. The opening of the vestry door followed by footsteps, the swishing of the metal thurible were easy to distinguish. The footsteps sounded again, and there was the rattle of chains as the vessel was hung up, followed by just a few footsteps, then the vestry door again, opening and closing. The figure's hand closed around the heavy stone that it had taken out of a mackintosh pocket.

Grasping this stone firmly, it crept over to the hanging thurible and, using a handkerchief, lifted it down, lifted the top, and slipped the stone in on top of the charcoal. It then took the vessel in its right hand, giving it an experimental swing back and forth to gauge its weight, then kicked at one of the pews to alert Silas that there was someone in the church.

'Is that you, Vicar?' he called. 'I've got the incense and the boat, and I'm all ready for you. Vicar? Vicar, is that you?' He wasn't so sure now but he ought to check. And if it was the vicar, he could collect his thurible to finish the ritual, which was something they needed to do together. The vicar would need to take the boat, and bless the incense before spooning it in on top of the glowing charcoal.

'Vicar?' he called one last time, and decided that he really ought to find out who was in the church, in case it was someone with mischief in mind. He wasn't far wrong there, as things turned out. He opened the vestry door and stepped out and, as he did so, was aware just for a split second of a heavy whirling sound, a sharp pain on the temple, and he knew no more.

As the robed man crumpled to the stone floor, the figure removed the stone, now a little warm, from the thurible, hung the metal vessel back up where it had been, then moved quickly and silently back to the choir vestry where it retrieved the mackintosh. Leaving the church wearing the already rain-splattered item, it merely walked a short way down to the junction with the High Street, going down a few more yards before stopping and taking up a waiting position again, in the only place possible in which to shelter.

Rev. Florrie, aware that she needed to be at the church in time not just to greet her congregation, but to bless the incense for the thurible and slip into her service robes, left the house about a quarter of an hour before the service was due to start, knowing that nobody but poor old Silas would leave any earlier than they had to, what with the downpour.

Almost immediately her umbrella was blown inside-out, and she fought with it all the way round to the church door which was, as expected, unlocked and left ajar, a thoughtful touch of Silas' considering the awful weather.

As she dumped the remains of her crazily shaped umbrella, she mentally renamed it an un-brella. Putting her head inside the church, she called out, 'Silas? I'm here. Are you ready for me?' Smiling at how salacious this could sound to the wrong ears, she suddenly became aware that all she had heard in return was her own voice echoing round the empty stone building.

She was almost certain he would have heard her from where she had been standing, but put the lack of response down to the acoustics of a building with which she was not yet very familiar. She entered the church which was dark from the sudden appearance of storm clouds, switching on the electric lights as she went. Looking round, she caught sight immediately of the thurible hanging from its accustomed nail, so everything looked as it should be.

And then there was Silas, all robed up and lying on the floor in a pool of blood from his head wound, and nothing was as it should be. Throwing off her raincoat, she rushed to his side and knelt down on the hard stones beside him. 'Silas?' she urged him. 'Did you have a fall or something? What happened?'

Silas had no comment to make to any of these questions about his state of health, because he no longer possessed a state of anything. 'Silas? Silas?' she urged him, shaking him by the shoulder to try to rouse him.

Finally, putting her fingers to the pulse point on his neck, she realised that he was dead, and the only thing she could do for him now was pray. Putting her hands together, she began, 'O lord, we deliver this soul into thy care this day …'

Dammit, she should ring the police. She could pray for

Silas' soul after they had been informed of this third death, but this one must surely be an accident. He must have fallen and hit his head on the stone floor. Church buildings were very unforgiving, if one had the misfortune to have an accident in one.

And what in the name of all the saints was she going to do about the service. It was due to start soon, and within minutes, people would be arriving. Going back to her raincoat, she removed her mobile and phoned DI Falconer, whilst stationing herself in the porch, with the door closed behind her.

This was not going to be an easy job, she thought, knowing that Sylvia Slater would be one of those arriving, expecting the unusual experience of singing with the choir. However would the poor woman cope? They had no children, and she would be all on her own now. Then she saw the woman approaching, all smiles and chatting with Polly Garfield. Florrie could feel a favour from Marjorie Mundy coming on.

As the straggle of choristers and congregation neared the church, thunder exploded like artillery, lightning went all out for a Hammer Horror audition, and Florrie stepped to the front of the porch, indicating that they could come in with her, but would get no further.

She held up her hands for silence, and explained, calmly and simply, that there had been an accident, and she was waiting for assistance. Service this morning was cancelled due to unforeseen circumstances, and would they accept her sincere apologies, not just for the cancellation, but for the lateness of this announcement. She urged them to go back home, and she would send news later of what had happened, if the village grapevine didn't beat her to it.

They all dispersed in a rush to avoid getting any wetter than they already were. Except, that is, for Sylvia Slater, who stood there in silence, before asking. 'It's something to do with my Silas, isn't it? What's happened to him?

Have you called an ambulance?'

Florrie, with an expression of great sadness, told her that Silas was now beyond anything an ambulance crew or hospital could do for him, and she burst into noisy tears, crying openly like a child, with her hands at her sides. 'I want to see him,' she finally blurted out. 'Do you know what happened?'

'I'm afraid I don't. I hadn't arrived when he had his accident, so I don't know how it happened.' Leading her gently by the hand, she took her in to see her husband's body. 'He's in a better place now, Sylvia,' intoned Florrie, hoping that her faith might provide the woman with some comfort.

'He'd just decided to wallpaper the spare bedroom – heaven knows it needs doing. And he always hated decorating, but this is taking avoidance a bit far.' Sylvia had used this flippant statement to help deal with her shock and grief. Silas was supposed to be here with her for years to come yet here he was lying dead on the stone floor of the local church they had attended all their married life.

'Come on. I'm going to take you to Marjorie Mundy's, and let her look after you for a while. I've informed DI Falconer, and he'll bring whoever's necessary with him and have a good look round to see if he can see what happened. Here, take my arm. The rain's left off a little bit now, and it's only a few steps.'

Locking the church door behind them so that no nosy parker could sneak in to see what all the fuss had been about, she delivered Sylvia Slater to Eyebrows, explaining briefly what had happened, then saying that she must rush as she was expecting the police. Gently handing over the grieving woman to the wheezing one, she made a dash back to St Cuthbert's just as Falconer's car pulled up outside.

As the three of them made a dash for the church porch,

Falconer shouted through nature's tympani section, 'What have you got for us this time, Rev. Florrie?'

'I am becoming a bit of a regular,' puffed Florrie, who wasn't used to running. 'It's Silas Slater, our thurifer. I think he's had an accident. But he's definitely dead.'

Once inside the building, they shed their outer garments, and Carmichael shook himself like a dog, more out of habit than because he was wet. Falconer looked over at him and thought his sergeant had spent too much time with dog breeders and their animals.

Rev. Florrie held out a pointing finger, but Silas' chasuble was so pale that he was easily identifiable on the church floor, once you knew what you were looking for. 'I thought he'd fainted. Then I thought he'd had a fall, then I checked his pulse. He must have hit his head on the floor and just had the bad luck to hit it at an unlucky angle,' she told them.

The inspector got down on his hands and knees to look over the body, while Carmichael remained upright. Both men had donned gloves as soon as they had entered the building. As Falconer examined the body, Carmichael cruised thoughtfully round the area where Silas' body lay.

'There's no real mark here where he could have hit his head, but if he bled on the spot, there wouldn't be,' said Falconer. 'What are you doing, Carmichael? Why aren't you down here with me?'

The sergeant was standing by the hanging metal vessel, looking all round it with great interest. 'I think I've found something, sir,' he said, suddenly showing signs of excitement.

'What's that?'

Rev. Florrie sat down in a pew and left them to it. Her whole body had now begun to shake, and she didn't know if it was this particular death that had got to her, as she was getting to know Silas as her thurifer, or whether it was the accumulation of the three deaths that had occurred in only ten days. Wrapping her arms around her body to try to quell her tremors and get warm again after the rain outside, she tuned out what was happening at the front of the church, and thought, instead, of happier times.

Falconer got to his feet so that he could examine what Carmichael had found, and the sergeant pointed out a slight imperfection in the shape of the thurible, hanging there so innocently on its nail, and tiny traces of blood at one corner.

'Rev. Florrie,' called the inspector. 'What was this object doing hanging here?'

Breaking out of her reverie about her happy childhood, the vicar looked at what he was indicating and explained, 'By the time I arrived, he would have got the charcoal alight in it, and he would have been waiting for me to arrive to bless the incense and spoon it in. Once it's alight, it's left outside the vestry on that old nail until I'm ready for us to proceed.'

'So he'd got his robe on and done all the preparation … Is it all right if I take this down to have a look inside?'

'Help yourself. Silas won't be swinging it now. There's no service to have need of it.'

Reaching it down he lifted the top, moving it up the chains, and saw a slightly glowing ember of charcoal inside but it seemed to be very flat. 'Would you mind coming to have a look at this?' he called to the vicar.

Florrie rose and approached them on legs that seemed more jelly than flesh and bone. Peering inside the vessel, she said with surprise, 'It does rather look as if it has had something on top of it, and it's not glowing as much as it should be. It should be red-hot by now.'

Careful not to disturb it, he showed her the base where there was slight damage and he had noticed the traces of blood. 'Good work, by the way, Carmichael. That was real out-of-the-box thinking.'

'Is that a good thing, sir?'

'Yes, of course it is.'

'Then, thank you.'

'Do you think you could take the vicar home and get down a statement from her while I call for back-up? This was no accident. This was murder, and rather a clever one at that – just not quite clever enough.'

A look of relief crossed Florrie's face as she realised she would not have to spend any more time in the church with poor Silas' mortal remains, and she took Carmichael's arm gladly. Before they left, Falconer asked, 'By the way, where's his wife?'

'Where I'd just been taking her when you arrived. At Marjorie Mundy's, Eyebrows, Pig Lane, just after the vicarage; you remember?'

'Can you go there afterwards, Carmichael, and speak to the widow, then ask her if she wants anyone contacted, or to be taken anywhere where there might be sympathetic company.'

'Will do, sir.' And thus they set off. Florrie was only a small woman and from behind their walk looked really comical, Carmichael skipping a step now and again to keep down to the pace of her so much shorter legs.

Falconer began to prowl round the church while he waited for a forensic team and Doc Christmas to arrive. When the pathologist did get there, he arrived at just about the same time as the rest of the scene of crime crew, and waited patiently for photographs etcetera to be taken before he could 'haul the body about a bit', as he described what he did at a crime scene.

When Christmas finally got his hands on the body, he confirmed the preliminary suggestions of the two detectives, and the thurible was packed away as evidence and removed from the church.

The rest of the building had given up only one clue, and this was a pool of rainwater on the choir vestry floor. It was evidence of the presence of someone else in the building that morning, and probably indicated what the murderer had done with his or her coat whilst preparing to take a life.

The 'boat' was laid out in the vestry, identified by Falconer by what Rev. Florrie had told them, along with the incense. Silas' raincoat was on a hook, but there was no evidence of anyone else having been in there. They didn't have much to go on so far, but they had, at least, identified the murder weapon. He'd get Roberts on door-to-door to see if any of the neighbours saw anyone out and about between the time that Silas left home, which he'd get when Sylvia's statement was taken, and also the time Rev. Florrie arrived. That would give them a time frame.

The biggest conundrum was why: why had these three particular people been killed, and were they in fact all killed by the same person? Were one or more of the murders a blind to disguise the real victim and confuse the issue, or was there reasoning behind it all?

He had no idea of the answers to these questions, and knew this case would take a lot of unravelling. They had four men to take in for questioning tomorrow, and that might prove crucial to their investigations. On the other hand, they might be barking up the wrong tree completely.

When Carmichael made it back to the church, the rain had reduced to a shower, and as they left the village, Carmichael asked, 'Would you like to come back to ours for a cup of tea, sir?'

Falconer was about to refuse vehemently, remembering his ruined trousers from the day before, then he remembered his last visit, and the fact that Harriet, whom he had actually delivered just after Christmas the previous year, did not seem to know him any more, and he had promised himself that he would see more of the children, especially as he was godfather to all three of them.

'Only if you promise to put Mulligan out into the back garden,' he eventually replied.

'No sooner said than done, sir,' replied Carmichael, grinning. 'Sir?'

'Yes, Carmichael?'

'How come we never get to swan around with take-away cups of coffee like all the cops on the telly?'

'Because we only get to investigate in the boondocks, Carmichael. Where have we ever been on a case where there was such a thing as a coffee shop? And if there had have been, we'd never have thought of it because we never get the opportunity to "swan about", as you so descriptively put it, with a nice hot drink.'

Kerry opened the door to them and gave them both a beaming smile, looking even more swollen than before. Falconer briefly thought that if the twins were to take after Carmichael in their build, then she'd have a hard time giving birth, then admonished himself at having such a thought from what must be his feminine side, something he had never before considered he possessed.

As they walked into the house, there was a deep whine of joy from the kitchen doorway, and Mulligan thundered over and put his huge paws on his favourite inspector's shoulders. Falconer staggered backward, desperately trying to keep his balance, until he lost the unequal fight and fell backward, fortunately, into a handily placed armchair, where Mulligan proceeded to attempt to lick his face off.

The Carmichaels' two little dogs saw the fun, and soon he had Mistress Fang defending him from his right trouser leg, and Mr Knuckles carrying out a similar action on his left. Dipsy Daxie, not wanting to be left out of the fun, but finding that there were no opportunities in the trouser leg department, scrambled up into the inspector's lap and collapsed with a wheeze of contentment. It was like wearing a living draught excluder.

Carmichael came cantering over, his approach not unlike the shambling gait of the colossal dog's, and hauled

171

at Mulligan's collar to remove him, before putting him out into the back garden, from whence he whined piteously to be let back in to play with his friend.

'Cup of tea?' called Kerry, from the kitchen door, as Falconer fought to remove the handkerchief from his trouser pocket.

'No thank you,' he replied, with as much dignity as he could muster. 'I've just had a pint of saliva.'

'I'm so sorry,' she said, approaching him with a roll of kitchen paper.

'Carmichael, I thought you said you'd put him out in the garden,' barked Falconer, somewhat tetchily, and fighting the need to retch.

'I did, sir. But I could hardly do it before we got here.'

'And you didn't think to phone ahead and get Kerry to put the big lug outside?'

'Um, no. Sorry, sir.' He was silent for a few seconds, then defended his lack of action by adding, 'It was still raining then. It's stopped now, so he won't get drenched out there. You wouldn't believe the mess he can make when he gets wet and comes indoors and shakes himself.'

Mm, thought Falconer, a bit like you when you got into the church.

The boys, who had been playing upstairs, heard the rumpus and came clattering down crying, 'Uncle Harry's here!' Even young Harriet, interested in the person who was at the centre of all the fuss, crawled over to have a look, and Falconer, after such an unpromising start to his visit, began to get to know the children again.

Before he left, Carmichael took him aside and said, 'I certainly needed my headgear today, didn't I, sir?'

'Indubitably, but do you think you could find something different to wear to the office tomorrow? A baseball cap is not really suitable for interviewing suspects in cases of serious crime.'

'Will do, sir. See you in the morning.'

The only thing in Falconer's mind at that moment was, 'I must have a shower. I must have a shower. I must have a shower. And I think I might be sick.'

Chapter Fifteen

Monday Morning

The skies had cleared, and the sun had poked its head out again with the promise that, maybe they could have a few more days of good weather before it disappeared behind the curtain of cloud that announced autumn. Its act was nearly at an end, but it had come back for just one more encore.

Falconer was, as usual, first into the office, and sat at his desk musing about the busy day that lay ahead of them. Their appointment with the chief planning officer was for nine thirty that morning, those with the councillors for four and four thirty.

That would give them time, thought Falconer, to pick up Mr Pooley after their first appointment and question him for a while and, if necessary, leave him sweating in a holding cell while they picked up Grimble and Smallwood, then Rev. Monaghan from Carsfold.

They could then conduct their other interviews and get back and split up, pairing with other officers to question the other three. There was enough computer evidence to put at least three of these into a muck sweat, and Rev. Monaghan might lie, but he might actually stick to the truth and the integrity of his calling.

He heard Carmichael enter the office and turned round, with no idea what to expect, remembering that he had told his sergeant to wear different headgear today. Well, he'd certainly done that. 'What the dickens is that on your head now?' he asked in a strangled voice.

'You told me to wear something different on my head, so I did and, as the sun was out, I've worn what I usually wear if we go to the seaside.'

'It's a knotted handkerchief!' squeaked the inspector. 'And just how do you think that's better than a baseball cap?'

'I don't, sir, but it's different. And one of Kerry's headscarves would have been too gaudy for your approval'

'I'll give you that. It's certainly different. Get it off now. I've got a flat cap in my car that you can wear when we go out, and you can jolly well keep it on for the rest of the day. On second thoughts, let me have a closer look at your scalp.'

Carmichael sat down, so that the inspector could reach his head, and removed the handkerchief with its four knotted corners. Falconer leaned over to take a close look, then gave a deep, deep sigh.

'I didn't look closely before. I thought henna tattoos were always of sort of tribal patterns and symbols,' he growled.

'They said I could have anything I liked,' retorted Carmichael with some petulance in his voice.

'So you got them to do Kojak and Columbo?'

'Why not?'

'You simply don't have the time to hear my reasons why you should never have had something like that. You're a real one-off. If I didn't know you better, I'd say you were a bit soft in the head. Now, ring Roberts and find out why he's late again, and tell him to get his arse straight in here because I've got a job for him.'

Feeling a little hurt, Carmichael did as he was told, and finished his phone call to inform the inspector that Roberts' alarm clock had broken, and he'd overslept. 'Did you tell Sleeping Beauty that I wanted him here *tout de suite*?'

'I did sir. He started to whine on about breakfast and a shower, but I told him to just get his skates on, and he could use the station's facilities and canteen when he had the time.'

'That's more like it. I'm sorry I snapped, just now, but sometimes you really infuriate me.'

'That's all right, sir,' replied Carmichael, mollified. 'Kerry says exactly the same thing.'

A bedraggled DC Roberts slammed open the office door and stalked to his desk looking very disgruntled. Before he could open his mouth to complain Falconer got in first.

'I need you to go over to Ford Hollow and call at all the houses in the High Street and Pig Lane to see if anyone saw someone hanging about in the rain between nine thirty and ten o'clock, anywhere near the church. Then I want you to see if there's anything back from forensics and check if the post mortem's been done. Oh, and I shall need both you and PC Green this afternoon for interviews.'

'But, guv,' moaned Roberts.

'Don't you dare "guv" me. You can grab a bacon butty from the canteen on your way out, then use the facilities here during your lunch break. I cannot put up with your persistent lateness, and I won't pander to you wanting to do everything as you would have done had you got out of bed on time.'

'Sorry, sir,' mumbled Roberts, heading back towards the door, his head bowed and a sulky expression on his face.

'Come on, Carmichael,' said Falconer, noticing the sergeant's apprehensive face. 'Don't worry, I'm not about to bite your head off now. We've cleared the air. Now, let's get to my car and sort you out that cap.'

The cap was a leather one, and Carmichael was delighted with it, even thought it was just a tiny bit small. The fit produced another deep sigh from Falconer, for it looked a bit like a pea on a mountain, but it was better than either the knotted hanky or the baseball cap, and when he'd had a close look at Carmichael's scalp, there were definitely small hairs fighting their way through the henna artwork, if such it could be called. Another week or so and he could go bareheaded and look as if he'd only had a number one at the barber's.

Mike Greenslade, the chief planning officer proved a pleasant man who, when asked if he knew about the protest about possible planning permission for a number of dwellings on the edge of Ford Hollow, scratched his head and answered, 'Um, yes. A bit.'

'Which bit?'

'That, um, some people were unhappy about it.'

'Did you know about the petition?'

'Um, can't remember. Ask me another.'

'Have you had any letters or phone calls about it?'

'Yes. Um, phone calls. Don't know about letters. You'd have to ask my secretary. Can't keep everything in the old napper.'

'And who were these phone calls from?'

'Um, let me see … a woman called, um … Poole, was it?'

'Pooley,' supplied Carmichael.

'That's the fellow.'

'She's a woman,' stated the sergeant, wondering if the man was going senile.

'I know. It was the name I was referring to. That was the fellow,' replied Mike Greenslade, wondering why the sergeant seemed to be having so much trouble understanding a perfectly simple situation.

Carmichael, still in the dark, decided it would be quicker and easier to stay out of it, rather than try to unravel the man's muddled thoughts about who was a man and who was a woman.

'And what did she say to you?' asked Falconer, noting that Carmichael had out his notebook and was scribbling away.

'Quite polite at first, then she turned nasty. Accused me of taking back-handers, which I understand are bribes. Well, I've never been so insulted in all my life. The world's gone mad. There are some cutbacks due, and I think I might volunteer for redundancy.'

'How many times did she phone you?'

'Two or three, then I started filtering my calls through my secretary, because she was getting very abusive.'

'Did you get phone calls from anyone else on this subject?'

'None that were put through to me. I'll take you through to Sandra, my secretary, and you can ask her about both calls and letters. I just get on with my job and try to keep out of trouble.'

Left with Sandra, she gave them much more information than Greenslade, pulling up about twenty letters, a few pleading for sanity, the others abusive and anonymous. She also said she had declined to put through several calls to her boss, and that there had been e-mail abuse as well, but she just deleted it.'

'That's a pity,' mused Falconer.

'I just didn't think about it at the time,' replied the secretary, with a shrug. 'Sorry.'

'Don't worry about it, Sandra. At least you kept the letters. People usually burn this type of correspondence.'

'They might have been needed in case the person who sent them caused a fuss. Anyway, we don't burn anything here. Everything physical is neatly filed for some unspecified time in the future, when the contents will prove vital for something or other. That's local government for you.'

'It's better than a cover up. Well done. Can we take them, please?'

'If you sign a receipt for them.'

'We'll return them as soon as we can. Many thanks for your foresight and cooperation.' Falconer couldn't see what good these anonymous communications would do the case, but at least it was something concrete, and might be of use to them.

They had had to return to the police station to get a pool car as Falconer's was a two-seater and, now in a more appropriate vehicle, they headed towards Ford Hollow. As they pulled up outside Wheel Cottage, Carmichael spoke. 'It would have been a lot easier if Roberts had made all three interviews for the morning. Neither councillor lives far from the council offices.'

'That's just typical of him. He probably made the appointment with Greenslade first, then found the councillors weren't available in the morning.'

'I bet he could have changed the one with the chief planning officer. He works office hours.'

'I think you're mistaking Roberts for someone who gives a damn, Sergeant. That would have meant another phone call, and he'd actually done what he was asked, so why should he think of the inconvenience of what he'd arranged?'

'You really don't get on with him, do you, sir?'

'I don't see him often enough to get on with him. If he's not on sick leave, he's off skiving somewhere.'

David Pooley looked grey and drawn when he answered the door to them, and was snappy with either tiredness, grief, or guilt. 'What do you two want again? I'm supposed to be picking up the children this afternoon, and I'll have to leave soon.'

'We need you to come down to the station with us to answer a few questions, sir,' declared Falconer.

'I've just told you I've got to pick up the children,' he

snapped back.

'Then you will have to change your arrangements, sir.' Falconer was firm.

'I have no intentions of doing that. You'll have to come back another time.'

'I'm afraid that won't do, sir. Either you come with us now voluntarily, or I'll have to arrest you.'

'This is outrageous!'

'This, sir, is a triple murder enquiry. It's not a parish picnic.'

'There's been another one? God, who was it this time?'

'Silas Slater, the thurifer. Will you please rearrange picking up your children and accompany us to the station. We'll be as brief as we possibly can.'

'I suppose so,' he agreed with ill grace, and tried to shut the door in their faces while he went to attend to this chore.

'We'll wait inside, if you don't mind, sir. Don't want you slipping out the back way and driving off, do we?'

'Don't be so ridiculous,' replied Pooley, pulling the door open wider and letting them into the house.

When they had gone through the procedure of booking him in at the station, they took Pooley to interview room number one. This was something that Falconer always enjoyed, for although they'd had an interview number one at the old station, they didn't have any higher numbers in which to interview other suspects.

Starting the tape, Falconer declared the date and time of the interview, who was being interviewed, and who else was present, which included PC Green, positioned just inside the door.

The inspector started with, 'How long had the affair been going between your wife and Xavier Smallwood?' It was blunt, but it got a reaction.

'I don't know what you're talking about,' blustered

Pooley, whose face turned from a strained grey to bright red.

'Yes you do, Mr Pooley. We found the emails on your wife's computer, and the replies on Smallwood's computer, which we also seized. Now, tell us how long it had been going on and what you did about it.'

'I don't know. I discovered the emails, but only after she was killed, and I had no idea who they were from. I was devastated.'

'I suggest that you found them before your wife was murdered, and they so infuriated you that they drove you to kill her.'

'That's nonsense. What would I do with the children while I was murdering their mother?'

Falconer nodded to Carmichael, and he took over. 'It would have been quite natural for them to have been playing at a friend's house on a Sunday morning. If that happened, it would have been quite natural for you to walk down to the church to meet your wife – assuming the children had not gone to Sunday school that day, which it is easy enough for us to check.'

Nice one, Carmichael, thought Falconer. Why had they not thought to check this out before? He'd have to ring Rev. Florrie and get her on to it.

'I told you, I didn't know anything about it before she was killed,' countered Pooley.

'And I don't believe you, sir,' replied Carmichael sternly.

'Why did you do it like that?' Falconer intervened. 'Was it because she spent too much time on her organ-playing and the choir, leaving you at home on your own a lot of the time and then had the infernal cheek to have an affair with another man? Do you work from home, Mr Pooley?'

'I do work from home, but I never resented the time she spent at the church.'

'And yet you never attended services?'

'I'm agnostic.'

'Not even to support your wife and hear the results of all her efforts?'

'I don't know. I feel uncomfortable in churches, where everyone seems to know what they're doing.'

Falconer nodded again to Carmichael, to indicate that he was taking over the ball again. 'So, if anyone said they had seen you near the church just before your wife was murdered, they would be lying?'

At this, Carmichael's head shot up, but the inspector shot him a small frown. OK, he was improvising, but it might produce results.

'I was at home. I never went out all morning,' Pooley spluttered.

'And can anyone prove that and give you an alibi? Your children perhaps?'

'They were playing with friends. I didn't collect them until after I was told what had happened.'

'And what about the abusive emails your wife received? Did you want to do something about that as well?'

'I never saw those, either, before she died.'

'Is there anything else you want to tell us or ask us, Mr Pooley?'

'Yes. You're surely not thinking I committed all three murders, are you?'

'Interview terminated at …' Falconer wasn't going to get drawn into that one. 'I'll arrange for someone to drive you home so that you can get off to collect the children, but we may need to speak to you again.

Back in the office, they found DC Roberts, his feet up on his desk, an open newspaper held out before him. Hearing someone coming into the office, he crumpled the newspaper down into the kneehole of the desk, and hurriedly pressed a button to awaken his computer, but Falconer had got a glimpse of him, and knew exactly what he had done.

'Got another job for you, Roberts,' he said. 'I want you to contact as many hotels, guest houses, and holiday letting agencies as you can, and see if they have any German guests, then report the results back to me. You can start now, but we'll need you for the first part of the afternoon to sit in on interviews. Are you having lunch in the canteen?'

'Yes, sir, and a belated breakfast.'

Showing no sympathy whatsoever, and convinced that the DC had managed to visit this facility and get some scoff while they were out, Falconer felt no sympathy. A quick glance in the wastepaper bin convinced him of this, when he caught sight of a sandwich packet, a yoghurt carton, an empty crisp packet, and an apple core, along with an empty cola can. Roberts had certainly got his breakfast in. Smart enough to get himself fed, but not smart enough to dispose of the evidence before making a play for sympathy.

'Come along, Carmichael. We'll leave Roberts to his task.'

As they walked out of the police station, Carmichael asked where they were going. 'Anywhere but the canteen,' the inspector replied.

'Is that why you asked him if he was going there?'

'No, I just wanted to confirm that he wouldn't be leaving the station before this afternoon. Knowing Roberts, I couldn't trust him not to be mugged. He might still go down with foot and mouth, or pustulating swine fever before we get back, though.'

'With what?'

'I made up that last one. I just don't trust him not to float off somewhere, or do something daft like go to the park then claim he has sunstroke.'

Monday Afternoon

After lunch in a local café, Falconer checked that Roberts hadn't made an attempt to escape, and they set off to interview the councillors who served on the planning committee.

The first one, Kenneth Carstairs, lived in a very grand house with a large garden and double garage. Carmichael's reaction only echoed what Falconer wouldn't have deigned to put into words. 'Cor, that's a bit flash, isn't it? Must've cost a bomb.'

A very smart woman who introduced herself as Mrs Carstairs answered the door to them, checked their cards and bade them enter. 'Kenneth's out in the back garden catching the last of the weather,' she told them, and walked ahead of them to show the way.

Kenneth Carstairs was enjoying the last of the weather – beside his in-ground swimming pool on a lounger, glass in hand. He looked round at the sound of their approach, and sat up suddenly, depositing some of the contents of his glass on to his lap. 'Sorry,' he said. 'I'd forgotten all about you coming.' Nice welcome!

As he led them indoors, Falconer muttered to Carmichael, 'It looks like he's taken a few back-handers in his time. I wonder if this place is called "Bung House"? Don't laugh. He'll want to know what I said.'

Carstairs didn't mince his words when they mentioned Yvonne Pooley's name, and went off into a tirade of invective about 'that interfering old bitch'. He'd had a lot of harassment from her, and had threatened to have a restraining order taken out against her. He'd heard she was dead, and was glad not to have to put up with any more of her interference.

'Yes, I've met her – unfortunately. What a harridan, and she was obsessed with stopping the planning permission being granted for the building of these houses at – where was it? – Ford Hollow. She had no idea how many jobs this would bring to the area, with more families moving to the village, they might be able to reopen the old village school, there would be more families living there; in fact, more life in general.'

'What about the disappearance of the ford and the diverting of a natural waterway?'

'A load of old sentimental, green, bleeding-heart liberal bollocks, in my opinion. If we all thought like that, there would be no towns or villages, and we'd still be living in caves. What a Luddite!'

'You don't believe that this proposed development is just a cynical money-making scheme, then?'

'Do you know what the pressure is for housing in this area alone? We need new development to cope with the burgeoning population.'

'Thank you for that, Mr Carstairs. Did you know anyone by the name of Albert Burton: an old man who lived in Ford Hollow?'

'Never heard of him.'

'What about Silas Slater, also a village resident?'

'Nope. Now, if that's all, I'll get back to my afternoon off in the sun, before it disappears till spring, if you don't mind.' These last words were uttered in a very sarcastic voice. The man evidently felt affronted that he should have been questioned at all about anything. Surely, he was fireproof against the everyday world?

The other councillor, Victor Dibley, lived in a much more modest Victorian house which was detached, but only just. He answered the door himself and asked them in, enquiring if they'd like a cup of tea, as he was about to have one himself. He may not have the grand residence that their last interviewee enjoyed, but he looked a much happier man.

They accepted his offer of refreshment, and settled

down in his homely sitting room which faced south, and got the best of the sun. 'Here we are then,' said a voice, and he came in with a tray laden with three chipped mugs, a large sugar bowl, and the milk bottle, without benefit of a jug.

'Excuse the crockery,' he apologised as he put his load down on a coffee table. 'Got a bit sloppy since the wife left me.' It sounded sad, but he said it with a smile, as if her departure had been a relief. 'Now, what can I do for you?'

As soon as they mentioned the proposed development at Ford Hollow, his face clouded, and he asked, 'Is this about the death of that Pooley woman? Shocking thing, that. Who could kill a woman with two children in the prime of her life?' He took a breath, and then enquired, 'Do you always take that much sugar, Sergeant?'

'Yes,' said Carmichael, quietly. 'What do you know about Mrs Pooley?'

'She came here once, you know, to have a go at me about that proposed building project.'

'What happened?'

'I asked her in for a coffee, and we sat and talked. I hate the destruction of natural habitats and tampering with nature unless it's absolutely necessary, and I don't agree with the building work proposed for that village. It's not just diverting the stream; the village hasn't got the infrastructure to cope with an influx of people on that scale.

'There's no surgery, no school, no shops, and now they're proposing to cancel the scant bus service that only runs one day a week. That's what she should have been protesting about. No supermarket will deliver out there, and they're going to be marooned if they haven't got their own transport.'

'And what did she say to that?'

'She said she'd get on to the bus company right away to

protest, and get a petition going for that as well.'

'How did you find her, sir?'

'I just opened the door, and there she was. Oh, sorry, I shouldn't be flippant about this: it's a serious business. I found her perfectly pleasant and easy to talk to, and what she said made a lot of sense. That land's been prone to flooding for donkey's years, and if they divert the water, it's only going to make its own way back again. Anything built there would be prone to flooding every time we had really wet weather.'

At last, a sensible opinion, not over-shadowed by personal gain, greed, or sentimental emotion, thought the inspector. 'I'd like to ask you if you have ever met anyone by the name of Albert Burton? Or, perhaps, Silas Slater?'

'No, sorry. I can't recall either of those, either in my personal or council life. I can't help you there.'

'Thank you very much for your time, sir: and thank you for the tea. It was very welcome.'

'And you make sure you brush your teeth properly, young man, taking all that sugar,' he said, as he waved goodbye to them at the front door.

'Where to now, sir?' asked Carmichael. They still had the pool car, so Falconer told him they would go straight to Landbank Ltd to pick up the other two, before dropping them off at the station and going out again for Rev. Monaghan.

Chapter Sixteen

Still Monday afternoon

At Landbank Ltd, an unexpectedly sudden meeting with Sheridan Grimble – he of the abusive e-mails to Yvonne Pooley – had Carmichael stuffing his knuckles in his mouth to smother the laughter he felt bubbling up at the sight of the man's nose again. Surely it was attached to the glasses, as were the moustache. He couldn't look like that by choice?

When told of their intention to take him in for questioning with regard to the abusive e-mails, his nostrils flared with anxiety, and he said, 'I hope you're not even going to think of prosecuting me about this. It would cripple the firm if I were out of action.' At this nasal movement, Carmichael took himself off to the lavatory where he could have a quiet laugh in peace before the tears rolled down his face.

Ignoring his sergeant's desertion, Falconer carried on regardless. 'We'll leave everything until we get to the station, sir. We need another of your colleagues as well.'

Xavier Smallwood was more sanguine, knowing that it was not possible to take any action against someone who had merely had an affair with a married woman.

With their first two interviewees in the car, the detectives returned to Market Darley to get them booked in before going to Carsfold to pick up Rev. Monaghan. Before they left the building again, however, Falconer decided to check that Roberts was still on the case.

He found him at his desk, but when he turned round at hearing the inspector's entrance, he proved to have a black eye and a split lip. 'What the hell's happened to you?' Falconer asked, surprised that his DC wasn't swinging the lead down at the local hospital again, and vaguely disturbed that he might have had a premonition earlier on.

'I got mugged, OK?' As Roberts assumed a pained expression, it gave Falconer leave to wonder if he was turning psychic.

'When?' asked Falconer, puzzled that his DC would have been out of the building. Surely he hadn't been set upon actually inside the police station. 'How? Where?'

Roberts sighed and began his sorry tale. 'I nipped out to the supermarket for some ciggies, because I'd nearly run out, and I was attacked on the way out of the place.'

'So what happened?'

'You might not believe this, sir, but that Sutherland woman – not the mother – was just going in to do her shopping, and she sorted out the attackers. Two of them, there were, and she pulled them off me and knocked their heads together.'

'Good grief! That dried-up old spinster? And did you recognise either of your attackers?'

'Yes, it was her, and no, I didn't recognise them. It was just a couple of young thugs who took me by surprise.' That's the main feature of muggings, thought Falconer. You don't know they're about to happen. 'But it's the final straw for me, sir,' the DC continued. 'I've put in a request for an immediate transfer back to Manchester. I've still got some annual leave left, so I'll use that to get my house on the market and get my personal stuff packed up. I'll probably rent it out for now. Then I'll get myself up there and look for somewhere to live while I think about the rest of my career.'

Falconer was stunned with this news. Roberts might be off sick a lot of the time, and not much use when he was in the office, but he was better than nothing, and there was a triple murder to solve.

At this point, Carmichael ambled into the office to see where the inspector had got to. 'Blimey, Roberts, you don't hang about when you've made your mind up, do you?' he commented when told the news.

'I'm going to speak to Superintendent Chivers,' declared Falconer, leaving the room abruptly. 'I can't be doing with this,' and he walked stiffly out of the room.

Superintendent Derek 'Jelly' Chivers was very surprised when an incandescent Falconer burst into his office without even the grace to knock. 'I simply won't stand for it, and you've got to get me a replacement immediately. I can't be one officer down when we've got three murders on our hands. It's hard enough to investigate with Roberts on the team, but without him, it'll be well nigh impossible and, meanwhile, time is passing, and we're not getting very far.'

Chivers told him to sit down and explain himself a little less hysterically. This was so unlike his usually almost monosyllabic inspector that he was concerned rather than angry.

'I'll see to it straight away, Inspector. It simply didn't cross my mind when Roberts' transfer was put on my desk by the man himself. He looked as if he'd taken a bit of a pasting, and I knew you and he didn't get on and how much sick leave he'd had since he joined us.

'I just thought you'd be pleased that he was going, and not getting under your feet again. I shall certainly be glad not to have him on my budget when he spends more time on his back than a prostitute. I'll get you someone immediately.'

'Thank you, sir.' Falconer stood almost to attention and left the superintendent's office, wondering how much pie-crust there was to his promise.

In the pool car again, on their way to Carsfold this time, Carmichael's jaw fell open with incredulity when Falconer told him what he'd said to the superintendent. 'And he didn't rip you to ribbons?'

'No, I think I made my point so forcibly that he realised how difficult it would be with one officer down and so much to do.'

'And he said we'd get someone else immediately? When do you think that will be?'

'Christmas? I don't know. For now, I'm going to hope that he meant what he said. We really are hard pressed. Ah, here we are.'

Rev. Monaghan's long-suffering wife answered the door, her body showing evidence of her latest pregnancy. Her hair was all over the place, and she looked tired and drawn. When they told her who they were, she said, 'I suppose it's about these murders in Ford Hollow. He's in his study. I'll just go and get him for you. Would you care to step into the hall?'

As they waited, the evidence of a crowded and chaotic household was all around them in the large, square space, with training shoes, school shoes, and Wellington boots all along one wall in a chaotic display, the opposite one covered in an array of coats which hung from a long series of hooks. School bags were dumped underneath these, and Falconer suddenly realised how much time they had used up this afternoon, with his unscheduled visit to the superintendent's office after Roberts' shock announcement.

When the head of the team ministry finally deigned to appear, they noticed that there was evidence of egg yolk and tomato ketchup down the front of his cassock which looked unbelievably grubby. Could one machine wash those things, or did they have to be dry-cleaned? wondered Falconer. He would have to ask Rev. Florrie.

'We'd like you to accompany us to the police station in Market Darley to answer some questions,' stated the inspector baldly, assuming that the reverend gentleman's wife had explained who they were.

'I don't see why I should do that. What have I got to do with any of this?' barked the vicar harshly, his face scowling from under his heavy eyebrows. If a person could look like Marjorie Mundy's cottage, Rev. Monaghan had just achieved this feat.

'We have received a phone call telling us that you were seen in the vicinity of St Cuthbert's church at the time the first murder was committed, and we would like to question you about it.'

'Can't you do that here?'

'No, sir. We would like to conduct a recorded interview with you under caution; for the record.'

'But I've got a PCC meeting to attend this evening. Why should I go with you?'

'Because if you don't, we shall arrest you, if necessary. I suggest you either cancel and reschedule your meeting, or get someone to deputise for you.'

'This is most inconvenient,' he snapped at Falconer, and called his wife back to the hall. 'Can you phone everyone on the PCC and say that the meeting will be on Wednesday night, not tonight. It seems that I am needed to help the police with their enquiries.'

His wife's expression changed from that of a person being put upon for the umpteenth time, to one of pleasure at getting a bit of unexpected time without him.

'Will do, Jude. You get on. I can manage perfectly well here.'

They'd probably done her a favour, as she would, no doubt, have been expected to rustle up the refreshments for the members wherever the meeting was to be held.

Rev. Monaghan behaved fairly well while being booked in

but, after being informed that he would have to wait some time until he was interviewed, he was not cooperative at all, and was finally dragged off to cool down in a cell, alternately swearing and farting in protest.

'Now you know why he's known as Old Bells and Smells,' Falconer informed Bob Bryant, who had looked on with interest at the unusual sight of a clergyman in the police station, apparently resisting arrest.

It was now time to interview the two men from Landbank Ltd, and Falconer sent Carmichael off to fetch DC Roberts and PC Merv Green, as they would take one each and would need a second officer present.

Green arrived looking excited at the prospect of being in on something as exotic as being the second officer interviewing. Roberts arrived a little more reluctantly, looking rumpled and battered and scowling at anyone who looked his way.

Falconer decided to interview Grimble, as he knew well Carmichael's reaction every time he saw the man, and allotted Smallwood to the sergeant, along with Roberts. Green he took with him and they went to collect their interviewee.

Sitting down at the table in the interview room – Falconer had selected room number two, just for the hell of it – he noticed that Green could not keep his eyes off Grimble's face. Knowing what was attracting his attention so irresistibly he gave the man a small kick on the ankle, but this only reduced the constable to giggles. Surely the man didn't have to look like that. He could have chosen rimless spectacles and shaved off his moustache?

'I'm sorry about my PC, Mr Grimble, but he's not used to interviewing, and he's nervous,' Falconer apologised lamely.

'He's laughing at my nose,' stated Grimble flatly. 'Don't worry, I'm used to it.' He didn't know the half of it.

Falconer cleared his throat, got Green to start the

recording, and made the necessary announcements to start the questioning. 'On your computer we found that you had sent abusive e-mails to Yvonne Pooley. These were also present on her machine. What do you have to say about what you did?'

'I didn't mean any harm,' began Grimble. 'I just meant to scare her off any more protest and fuss. If we don't get this land sold, we have a caveat in our contract to the sellers that we guarantee to sell their plot within five years of purchase, or we will refund the money.'

'Whatever made you do that?'

'Times were hard, and we didn't think we'd ever be able to shift the plots, but although things are getting better, it's vital that we sell them on before taking on any other projects, and we need to do that so that we make some money.'

'How long has Landbank been in operation?' asked Falconer, now intrigued.

'This is our first project together. If we fail at the first hurdle, we're finished, and we'll be up to our ears in debt for the lease on the office accommodation.'

'Oh, dear me. You are in a pickle, aren't you? So you thought you'd intimidate the woman to make her go away and stop being a fly in the ointment,' stated Falconer using all the clichés he could think of that were apt.

'In a word, yes,' agreed the walking nose. Green giggled again and earned a scowl from the inspector.

'Did you threaten her with physical violence?'

'You know I did if you've read the emails. I don't know what I'm going to do.'

'Did you ever meet her and offer her violence, or make threats to her face?'

'No. I never knew what she looked like. When I heard the name of the dead woman, I nearly wet myself.'

'And you didn't know either Albert Burton or Silas Slater?'

'No, I don't know many people around here. I only moved down when the four of us got together, and I spend most of my time working on site plans and only socialise with my colleagues. I really don't have a lot of friends.'

'You're absolutely sure about that? You are under caution.'

'I am,' said Grimble, grimacing, seeming to answer the question and confirm the statement in two words.

'I'm going to have a word with my superior about you. You will be charged with threatening behaviour, but as it was not in person, I think I might be able to get the charge to lie on the book for now.'

'God, I'd be so grateful. When you came for me this afternoon, I nearly dirtied my pants, wondering if I was going to go to prison.'

'Let this be a lesson to you, but I'm not promising anything. You can wait in your cell until DS Carmichael has finished with your colleague, then I'll get a car to take you back to your offices.'

Outside, he just looked at Green, who slipped effortlessly into abject apology, then started to giggle again. 'You must admit, that was a huge conk he had, sir. And those glasses and the moustache. I got something like that in my Christmas stocking one year, and I wet myself laughing when my dad put it on.'

Carmichael and Roberts, meanwhile, were learning the ins and outs – not literally, fortunately – of the affair that Smallwood had had with Yvonne Pooley.

'How did you meet?' asked Carmichael, after heading up the tape with everyone's details and the date and time.

'It was actually on the land itself at Ford Hollow. I was there in my capacity as surveyor, and she heard about my presence and came along to have an argument with me.'

'And did she?'

'Yes, an absolute beezer of a row. It was so full of genuine passion that we ended up kissing, and that was it.'

'What did you do?'

'We went back to her place. Her husband was at a conference, her children at school, and if anyone saw me, she could say that she'd kidnapped me from the proposed development site to give me a piece of her mind. As it turned out, she gave me a lot more than that.'

'That's quite enough detail, sir. Did her husband find out about you?' the sergeant continued. Roberts was having no part of this interview, and sat sulkily chewing his fingernails. Carmichael wasn't bothered. It was the first time he'd been left alone – as good as – to conduct an interview without Falconer leading the questioning, and he was relishing the opportunity.

'I don't believe he did, no,' answered Smallwood.

'How did you carry on with this affair if you were worried about being seen by the neighbours?' Carmichael asked.

'Easy. Whenever she had to come and do the shopping, she'd give me a ring, and we'd go to mine for an hour. There was always an excuse: bumped into an old friend and got talking, or went for a coffee, or there were very long queues. Her husband was engrossed in his work anyway, so she didn't need to make excuses often. He never noticed the time passing.'

'When was the last time you met?'

'About a week before she died – no, it was nine days, because it was on a Friday.'

'And you didn't have a falling out?'

'Not at all. If anything, things were getting more serious between us.'

'And you kept all this quiet from your colleagues?' asked Carmichael, now thinking that he was involved in his own personal soap opera.

'I had to. She was public enemy number one as far as they were concerned.'

Changing the subject slightly, Carmichael asked, 'And

was it your company's intention to use bribery to get what you wanted in the case of this particular planning application.'

'No comment. That's another matter altogether, and I wouldn't be willing to talk about it without my solicitor present.'

'Fair enough.' Which Carmichael was, and put this other matter on the back burner for a little bit of investigation after the murderer had been apprehended. He would also suggest that they take a look at the bank account of Councillor Carstairs. It might make very interesting reading.

When they had both finished with their interviewees, Falconer was as good as his word and organised a car to take them back to their offices, while they had Rev. Monaghan brought from the cell where he was waiting. The wait had not improved his temper, and he was very profane for a man of the church, thought the sergeant, his ears turning pink with embarrassment at the man's language.

'Now you have calmed down a little, Rev. Monaghan, we want to talk to you about information we received about you being in the vicinity of the murder scene shortly before Albert Burton was killed. That would be a week ago Friday between seven thirty and eight.' This was a little over-specific, but Falconer didn't care. He was fairly certain that the tipoff was genuine, and wanted to see how the man reacted.

It was with bluster, and an insistence that he be informed who had provided this information. 'I'm not at liberty to reveal our sources, Rev. Monaghan. I thought you would have realised that,' countered Falconer, and the man finally gave in and confirmed that he had, indeed been in Ford Hollow at about that time on the day in question.

'And what was your business there?'

This produced a couple of long minutes of silence, until he finally said, 'I skipped socialising after choir practice in my own church, and hurried off to see a little lady I visit on a fairly regular basis over there.'

Carmichael was scandalised, knowing that the man's wife was pregnant, but held his peace, his face getting redder and redder as his temper rose. First the man had cursed and sworn like a navvy, now he was admitting to being unfaithful to his wife, who was expecting their baby. He, of course knew this sort of thing went on, but what scandalised him most was that this was a man of the cloth who should be setting an example to others.

'We shall need her name and address so that we can confirm that you did actually go there, and what time you arrived and left. Don't look at me like that, Rev. Monaghan. I expect an answer, if I have to knock on every door in the village to find this woman who can vouch for you.'

'She's called Millie Foster, and she lives in Daffodil Cottage in Drovers Way,' he finally conceded.

'And why didn't you tell us this before?'

'It wasn't relevant at the time, and it's still not relevant. I had nothing to do with the murder of the old man.'

'Where were you the Sunday before last between about ten thirty and eleven?'

'Ditto,' replied the vicar, now showing slight signs of embarrassment.

'And this Sunday about nine thirty?'

'No dice, Inspector. I was in church preparing for service.'

'Which church?'

'Coldwater Pryors, as it happens.'

'Which is only a couple of miles from Ford Hollow. And, tell me, do you have a thurifer there who would be waiting for you to add incense to the thurible and bless it?'

'No. I haven't yet managed to convert that bunch of old

stick-in-the-muds to proper High Church services.'

'So you could have called in to St Cuthbert's before you arrived there and done for Silas Slater as well.'

'That is an outrageous suggestion. I did no such thing. Now I demand that you let me go, and I don't want to see you again unless you have a warrant for my arrest, which you won't obtain, because I'm innocent.'

'We had to let him go, Carmichael, but I shall be speaking to Millie Foster tomorrow. We'll go over there in the morning. I want to speak to Chelsea Winter again about finding Albert's body, in case anything else has come back to her. I also want to pop in and thank that Sutherland woman for rescuing our DC Roberts from the young thugs who attacked him earlier today.'

Back in the office, they found Roberts clearing his desk. 'It's all right, sir, no Germans to be found, not even under my desk.' Roberts had considered himself to be on a fool's errand, as an old soldier from the war was such an unlikely suspect, and there had since been two more murders, but he didn't care. He was going back to Manchester where the work had more adrenaline. There was not much excitement in interviewing a load of old turnips.

'You're actually going today?'

'No point in dragging it out. I won't say I've been happy here, but I'll drop in and see you if I've got to come back to sign documents relating to the house.'

'Good luck, Roberts.' Falconer held out his hand to be shaken, more with relief than anything else. He didn't wish the DC ill, but he'd be glad to be rid of him. Carmichael did likewise, and they saw him on his way.

'We'll have a case conference tomorrow, just the two of us. I'm sure we've got everything we need to know, but just haven't put the pieces together correctly. And don't think you're going to keep that cap when your hair grows back. I shall want it returned.'

'You'll be lucky,' said Carmichael, but he said it very quietly, so that the inspector didn't hear it.

Chapter Seventeen

Thursday Morning

Before Falconer could get anything done the next morning, his phone rang, and he found the superintendent on the other end of it. 'My office, now, Inspector,' was all he said before hanging up. 'Oh, God, what have I done now?' he said out loud, surprising Carmichael who was just entering the office.

'What's that, sir?'

'What the hell are you doing wearing your polo shirt back to front?' exclaimed Falconer, as he caught sight of what Carmichael was wearing and completely ignoring his question.

'I put it on back to front this morning, and Kerry said it would be bad luck to put it back the right way. My ma used to say exactly the same thing.'

'Well, if you think you're going out and about with me looking like you've got your body on back to front, you can think again. Turn it back the right way immediately, and don't go on about bad luck again. It's just a silly superstition.'

Carmichael did as bidden, then returned to the question he had asked as he had entered. What were you oh God-ing about?'

'I've been summoned on high to Jelly's office, and he didn't sound very pleased with me either.'

'Perhaps that vicar put in a complaint,' suggested Carmichael.

'He wouldn't dare – not with what he's been up to, and withholding information like that.'

There was a young man seated in the chair outside the superintendent's office, and Falconer vaguely wondered what he was there for, but concentrated more on what he himself was wanted for. He knocked gently and waited to be bidden to enter. He then stood straight as a ramrod, not daring to take a seat before, or even if, he was asked to. He was not.

'Inspector Falconer,' Chivers began in stern tones, 'I complied with your request yesterday about staffing levels, but on mature reflection, I have decided that I need to speak to you strongly about the way you worded your request. I have never been spoken to in tones like that in my life, and I do not intend to start now. You were abrupt, insubordinate, and downright rude –'

Falconer did not give him the chance to go any further. 'I wish to apologise unreservedly for my behaviour, sir, and assure you it will not happen again. I came up here in haste after Roberts had dropped his bombshell, and I should have thought about what I was going to say first.'

In lighter tones, Chivers replied, 'Thank you, Inspector, for your apology, which I accept – on the understanding that you do not act so rashly in the future. The other reason I wanted to see you was that there is someone that I would like you to meet.'

He rose and indicated that Falconer should follow him outside his office, where the young man he had noticed before now stood to attention. 'This is DC Tomlinson, who had already put in a request to join us here in Market Darley. DC Tomlinson, this is Inspector Falconer, under whom you will be working.'

The new DC held out his hand and said, 'I'm Neil. I've been waiting for a while to get a chance to come here. My girlfriend, Imogen, lives in the town, and we've been trying to sustain a long-distance relationship for some time.'

'DC Tomlinson won't be able to start today, as he came down by train last night, and needs to get himself sorted out,' explained Chivers, in case Falconer fostered any false hopes of the new DC starting right this minute.

'I'm moving in with my Imi,' said Tomlinson, with a wide grin and a wink, and Falconer took an instant liking to him.

'The DC is a sharp young man who will go far. I'm sure he will become an asset to your team,' finished Chivers, leaving them to it.

'Come along and meet DS Carmichael, who's also on the team,' invited the inspector.

'I'd love to.'

Carmichael was getting ready to set off for Ford Hollow and was just clearing his e-mails when they got to the office. 'Carmichael,' announced Falconer, 'this is DC Tomlinson, who will be working with us in the very near future. He's to be Roberts' replacement.'

Carmichael shook his hand, and Tomlinson reiterated his request to Falconer. 'Just call me Neil.'

'And I'm Davey,' replied Carmichael. They exchanged smiles.

'I'm moving in with my girlfriend. I just need to get my stuff sorted, and I'll be joining you in the office as soon as I can,' explained Tomlinson. 'At the moment we're arguing about wardrobe space, and I'm determined to obtain at least one drawer for my socks and a few centimetres of hanging space. Be seeing you,' and left the office to get on with things so he could get to work as soon as possible.

'I like him,' stated Carmichael, wearing his heart on his sleeve as usual.

'So do I,' agreed Falconer. 'Come on, let's get off for Ford Hollow before we lose any more of the morning.'

'And he didn't even ask why I was wearing a cap,' said

Carmichael, ending the short conversation.

'Who are we visiting?' asked Carmichael, as the Boxster schmoozed down the road to the village.

'I want to check with Chelsea Winter about finding Albert Burton, I want to drop in and thank Elodie Sutherland for coming to Roberts' rescue, and I'd like to drop in on Rev. Florrie, but we might leave that till this afternoon, as we've had the guts shot out of getting an early start on this. Oh, and we need to speak to that floozy of Rev. Monaghan's in Daffodil Cottage. What was her name?'

'Millie, sir: Millie Foster,' supplied Carmichael, who had been paying attention somewhere along the line.

'We're missing something, Carmichael, and I fear it's something obvious. I just can't think what it is,' sighed Falconer, absently.

They had decided to tackle Chelsea Winter first, provided she wasn't at school, and they were in luck, as the local school had an inset day. She was to be found upstairs in her room practising the new anthem and the seven-fold amen for the church choir to the accompaniment of an electric keyboard, which was placed on her bed. There was no room for it to sit on a stand, as the room was on the scale of the rest of the tiny house. Her parents were barely out of bed, and just pointed the way, both of them looking badly hung-over.

Chelsea sat in front of the instrument, on which she was practicing her parts. She looked up, startled, at the knock on the door, not expecting her parents to be bothering her at this time of the morning. 'Oh, hello,' she said, 'What do you want? I thought I'd given you a statement.'

Falconer's eyes had suddenly alighted on a couple of objects on the window ledge, and he was instantly distracted. 'Where did you get those?' he asked, trying not to stare too hard.

'The candlesticks?' she asked. 'They were a present from my boyfriend.'

'How generous of him. Who is he? Is he local?'

'He lives in Market Darley, but he's got a moped, so he can come over and fetch me.'

'What's his name?'

Looking a little nonplussed, she replied, 'John Hartley.'

'And what does he do? Is he still at school?'

Relaxing a little, at what seemed, now, to be genuine interest, she replied, 'No, he's left school and he hasn't got a job yet.'

Carmichael proved his weight in gold at this point, by asking, 'Whatever does he do with his time all day?'

'I think he drinks coffee and lager and watches telly,' she giggled.

'Would you excuse me a moment. I just have to go outside to make a quick phone call to confirm an appointment for this afternoon. What we would like would be to go through again what you remember about finding Albert Burton, and anything else you remember. DC Carmichael here will start off for a few minutes,' said Falconer, dropping an eyelid slightly in the ghost of a wink in Carmichael's direction.

The sergeant was puzzled, though quick on the uptake, and took over seamlessly, taking his notebook out of his pocket and thumbing through until he reached the right place. Falconer, meanwhile, took himself off outside and made his phone call.

'Is PC Green in the station?' he asked.

'As it happens, he's just dropped in for a break. Do you want me to get hold of him and put him on?'

'If it's not too much trouble.' He waited while the sounds of the station went on in the background. The switchboard, an old-fashioned item that had been an anachronism but still included when the new station was built, did not bother to put him on hold, as he was one of theirs.

It was only a couple of minutes before he heard the Essex tones of PC Green, who had probably been easy to find in the canteen, and he asked him if he had ever heard of a youth called John Hartley.

'A right young scallywag. We've got him on file for quite a few incidents, but no convictions yet. On the other hand, I think he's only seventeen years old, so give him time, is what I say.'

'Could you get over to his place? I have evidence that it was he who robbed DC Roberts' house, and I want his home searched particularly for a carriage clock, and him brought in for questioning. I shall be bringing in evidence that he certainly handled stolen goods when I get back.'

Returning to Chelsea's room, he found that Carmichael and Chelsea had finished the business end of the visit, and were now chatting generally, the sergeant relating particularly well to a girl of her age.

'Chelsea, I'm going to ask you a favour now. I'd like to borrow your candlesticks. I'll give you a receipt for them, but I need to check something.'

'Why?' asked the young girl.

'Because it's important, Chelsea.' Falconer didn't want to alarm her, being certain that she had received them as a gift in all innocence.

'I suppose,' she finally shrugged. 'They're a bit old-fashioned, aren't they?' she concluded and reached over for them.

'Let me do it. Can you go downstairs and see how your parents are? I was a bit worried about them when we arrived.'

'If you like, but they'll probably be on to the hair of the dog by now: and he's my step dad, not my dad.'

She went downstairs obediently as requested to do and Falconer slipped on a pair of gloves before removing the candlesticks from the window ledge and slipping them into an evidence bag, whilst explaining to his sergeant in a whisper, about his call to Green. 'You go down first and distract them, while I slip these out to the car. We don't want her phoning Hartley and alerting him before Green gets there, do we?'

'You what, sir?' asked Carmichael, who hadn't yet worked out what was going on.

'I believe these are the candlesticks from the robbery at Roberts' house, and I've got Green on his way to pick up the suspect, Chelsea's boyfriend, and look for the carriage clock,' he explained.

'Oh God, sir, it'll break her heart,' said the soft-centred sergeant.

'Better to do that now than later, when he goes to prison,' countered the inspector philosophically.

'If you say so sir.'

'I do. Now get downstairs and get them all into the kitchen on some pretext, no matter how flimsy. I don't want her to see the evidence bag, or she'll put two and two together. I'm surprised she hasn't already.'

'Do we need to take them straight back to the station?'

'I think they can survive locked in the boot of the car until we've seen the Sutherland woman, then we'll go back, and I'll make a proper appointment to speak to Rev. Florrie. To make sure she's going to be in. There's no point in us just dropping over, in case she's got a ladies' macramé group, or whatever it is retired church people do with their spare time. If she's not free it can wait. It's just a bit of a catch up really.'

As they pulled up in front of the Sutherlands' home, Falconer's mobile phone rang, and he answered it to find PC Green on the other end of the line. 'I've got him, sir, and the clock. He's in a cell waiting to be questioned. Have you got your evidence?'

'In my boot. We've got one more visit to make, then we'll be back, and you can confront him with what we've found, too: after they've been tested for fingerprints, of course.'

'He can wait, cocky little bugger,' replied Merv, grinning down the phone. 'He can hang on, kicking his heels until after I've had my lunch. He might be more ready to talk after a bit of time to think about things.'

'Good man, Green. We'll see you soon then.'

Lizanben looked depressingly respectable when they pulled up outside it. 'What about Millie Foster, sir?' asked Carmichael, as she seemed to have disappeared from their plans.

'I decided that she'll probably be at work, so we'll call on her when we come back later. She'll keep.'

As expected, Elodie Sutherland answered the door, coming over all smarmy when she saw who her visitors were. 'Do come in, gentlemen. What can I do for you today? Not another murder, surely? There have been three already.'

'Not at all, Miss Sutherland,' Falconer assured her. If we could come in?'

'Of course. Would you like tea?' she asked.

'Why don't we let my sergeant make it while I talk to you?' suggested the inspector.

'What a novel idea. The kitchen's this way,' she directed Carmichael, while showing Falconer into the living room where her mother sat watching a television set with the volume turned very low. Seeing him look at the old lady, she said, 'Don't worry about her. She's very hard of hearing anyway. The moving pictures keep her amused.'

Falconer sat down to the sound of clatters as his sergeant filled what sounded like an old tin kettle. 'We've come here to thank you for helping our DC Roberts,' he began, but was interrupted with what sounded like a fusillade of gunfire from the direction of the kitchen. 'Will you excuse me a moment. I just want to check that DS Carmichael isn't wrecking your domestic arrangements.'

Opening the kitchen door, he found Carmichael opening and closing cupboard doors and drawers in a frantic search for tea, cups, spoons, and teabags. 'Slow down, there. You sound like a Morecambe and Wise breakfast skit. Here, let me have a look,' Falconer admonished him.

'Cutlery drawer, under the draining board,' he directed, 'tea bags in the tin marked "Tea", cups and saucers in the wall cupboard to the left of the sink, sugar in the sugar basin, and tray down between these two cupboards. Oh, and I think you'll find the milk in the fridge. Now, do you think you can get a hot drink sorted?'

'Thank you, sir.' Carmichael was not used to the workings of a kitchen as he worked such long hours, and Kerry spoilt him rotten when he was at home.

Falconer took himself back into the strange time-warp that was the living room where the old lady still stared at the moving images on the television screen. 'I've pointed DS Carmichael at the right equipment to come up with a cuppa for us,' he told Elodie.

'Thank you so much, Inspector. It's such a novelty to have someone make me a cup of tea in my own home. I normally do everything, as Mother is so frail. Aren't you, Mummy?'

Mummy nodded her head without taking her eyes off the screen, and Elodie confessed that she might have to find a place in a nursing home for her elderly parent. 'She's getting a bit incontinent, you see, and I really can't cope with that on my own: I'm no spring chicken myself.'

'That will be a big change for you, won't it?'

'Oh, I have plans to keep myself busy, Inspector. Ah, here is your sergeant with the tea. Wherever did you find those mugs? I thought I'd put them away for good. Mummy used to like a mug, but since I've taken over the domestic arrangements, I've put them out of sight and got the good china out,' said Elodie, frowning at the crockery that Carmichael had selected. 'Never mind. It's just so nice to feel waited on. Thank you, Sergeant. I don't suppose you found the Earl Grey?'

'Who?'

'Never mind, Carmichael. Just put down the tray and sit down.'

'I didn't know we had titled people involved in this,' said the sergeant in all innocence.

'It's a type of tea, Sergeant. Don't bother about it,' interjected Elodie.

'My sergeant here couldn't find his own arse with both hands and a mirror,' declared Falconer, very out of character, drawing an exclamation from Carmichael.

'Sir!'

Falconer glared at him, indicating that he'd explain later.

As Carmichael sat down, looking rather hurt, and began to spoon sugar into his tea, Falconer carried on where he had left off before. 'As I said earlier, we're here to thank you for your intervention when DC Roberts suffered an attempted mugging. It was very brave of you.'

'I only did what anyone with a social conscience would have done,' she replied, sounding modest but insincere.

'It was an act of bravery that a lot of people, including most men, would have shirked,' replied Falconer honestly.

'I did do a little training when Daddy died,' Elodie admitted. 'I felt it was necessary with two vulnerable women living on their own. I'm just sorry I couldn't have stepped in a little bit sooner to stop the injuries he received.'

'Believe you me, Miss Sutherland, if you hadn't have intervened when you did, he could have sustained a lot more injuries.'

'I'm glad to have been of assistance,' she replied, again

flying the flag of false modesty. 'Just a moment – Mummy's dribbling tea all down the front of her cardigan.

'We must be on our way anyway. Thank you again for your public spiritedness, and thank you very much for the tea.'

'How is your colleague?' she asked, taking the mug from her mother and wiping her down briskly with a handkerchief.

Falconer had seen the ever-widening pool of liquid at Mrs Sutherland's feet, and it sure wasn't tea that was soaking into the carpet. It was time to make a diplomatic exit, without causing the woman any more embarrassment by showing that he'd noticed.

'He's fine,' replied Falconer, without enlightening her that this was just a guess as DC Roberts was no longer a colleague. 'We'll see ourselves out. Don't trouble yourself. See to your mother: she's much more important.'

When they were headed back to Market Darley, Carmichael raised a subject that had been playing on his mind since he had forgotten where the cups and saucers ought to be and unearthed the mugs. 'I think our Miss Sutherland must be going as batty as her mother,' he stated.

'Whatever makes you say that?'

'When I came across those mugs, there was a darned great stone in the cupboard with them. Very round and smooth, but hardly the sort of thing you put in a cupboard with mugs. Perhaps she's losing it.'

'Probably got too much to think about what with her church duties, doing all the cleaning, shopping, and cooking, and looking after her old mother. Or maybe it's used as a doorstop in high summer. I don't think that having a stone in her cupboard is proof of the onset of dementia, Carmichael. Her mother could have put it there?'

'She's far too old and short to do something like that.

And why did you say such a horrible thing to me about not being able to locate my own bottom?' His mother had never allowed bad language, and neither did Kerry, so he was used to watching what he said.

'I'm just getting a glimmer of an idea, so I'll leave it until it's a bit clearer before I explain myself, otherwise I'll get it all muddled up, and I won't be able to find my thread again.'

Chapter Eighteen

Tuesday Afternoon

When Falconer got back to his office, leaving Carmichael to get straight to the canteen as he was running short of fuel, he found his phone ringing. Rushing to answer it, he blurted out his name, and a female voice at the other end said, 'I'm phoning to find out if you've had any progress with finding Bonnie Fletcher.'

'And you are?' he asked, frantically ransacking his memory to locate the name and what it might have had to do with him.

'Bonnie, you know, from Robin's Perch,' she said, still not elucidating him as to what this was about.

'Whereabouts?' He was really struggling now. 'And you are?' he asked again, still frantically trying to place what this was about.

'Shepford St Bernard. Wanda Warwick,' came the answers.

'And what were we enquiring into?' He'd have to give up and ask for more details.

'Her disappearance in February. I was the friend who reported her missing, and I was wondering how you were getting on. You must remember me: the witch.'

Immediately she came to mind, and he could even picture the inside of her cottage, Ace of Cups. 'One moment,' he said, 'while I check the file.' A quick search of his computer pulled up very scant information. Unusually for missing persons, she had never been sighted anywhere, and the only things in the file were the initial interviews with her employer and her parents, apart from Wanda Warwick's.

'I'm afraid we've had no updates on the case almost since you reported her missing. Would you like me to do anything?' This was a naïve question, because of course she would expect action, but he had little idea what he could do to revive interest in the young woman's disappearance.

'She's been gone a long time, now, and I'm really worried about what's happened to her,' said Wanda, with genuine concern in her voice. 'What do you think happened to her?'

'A lot of people just up sticks and run off. Sometimes they have worries, real or imaginary, that make their life intolerable as it is, and they just want to leave everything behind. You wouldn't believe the number of people who just run off each year,' he replied, giving her a bit of soft soap.

'I'd never have considered that she'd do that, without even informing her parents.'

'Sometimes that's who people want to get away from. I'm afraid I don't have any information on her but, should something turn up, I will of course give you a ring. I have your number here on file.' Of this he was sure.

'I can understand someone not wanting to contact their parents, but I thought she would, at least, have contacted me.' Wanda's voice was now quite sad.

'Maybe she thought you'd tell her parents where she was, just to put their minds at rest.' Falconer thought he was winning now.

'Can I leave it with you, Inspector?' the woman said. 'I'm still very concerned for her safety.'

'You can rest assured that if anything turns up, you will be one of the first to know, Miss Warwick.'

'Thank you very much, Inspector. I hope to hear from

you in the not-too-distant future.'

She'll be lucky, he thought. Bonnie Fletcher is long gone, possibly mixing cocktails in somewhere like Kavos. He made a mental note to check for new evidence, but quickly dismissed Wanda Warwick from his mind as he heard footsteps enter the room and turned, expecting to see Carmichael – but he was wrong. 'Hello, DC Tomlinson,' he said, in surprise. 'I thought you were getting yourself sorted out.'

'I travel light, and I couldn't wait to get involved in a case. Can you let me know what you're currently working on?'

'I'll open the case file for you, and you can have a read while I nip to the canteen to see if DS Carmichael has left me anything to eat. I could do with a coffee and a bun before we go out this afternoon.'

'Thanks, sir, and do call me Neil.'

He found his sergeant ploughing his way across a large helping of shepherd's pie, chips, and baked beans, making his mouth water at the sight of his own secret sin, food-wise, and envisaging them smothered in brown sauce. 'Is that enough for you?' he asked, more in jest than anything else.

'No, but I've already had eggs, sausage, and chips, so this should see me through.

'You must spend a fortune in food each week.' This time, it was not a joke.

'I don't really know. Kerry sorts all that stuff out, and we're lucky that we're just inside the limit for supermarket delivery from Market Darley. Kerry orders it all online, she could never carry it herself.'

'I can believe that. I just thought I'd let you know that Tomlinson has reported for duty, and I've left him with the case notes. I'm going to order something and top up on my sugar level, then I'm going to try to secure us appointments for this afternoon. We want to speak to

Millie Foster, and I'd like to catch up with Rev. Florrie again.

'When you've finished, would you like to show Tomlinson round the station and introduce him to everyone? It would save me a job, and I can get on with those phone calls.'

'Will do, sir,' sprayed Carmichael, his mouth stuffed full of minced meat and potatoes.

When Carmichael returned to the office, Falconer had located Millie Foster in the telephone directory, and made an appointment for three thirty, as she only worked part-time, and one with Rev. Florrie for somewhere between three thirty and four o'clock. He had also made enquiries at the college of further education in Market Darley, to check up on a certain type of course, and who had signed up for them. The answer gave him pause for thought.

It also gave him just enough time to interview John Hartley, who had been stewing in a cell for some hours, now: PC Green had come up trumps, and the young lad must be close to cracking now he knew the candlesticks had been found, as well as the carriage clock that Green had removed from his mum's house.

It didn't take long to break him down far enough to confess to burgling DC Roberts' house, and to defacing the front door. 'I shoulda known better than to do over a pig's house,' he sighed, as he was asked to sign a written confession.'

'I don't think you're very good at this sort of thing, Hartley. Why don't you do yourself and us a favour by going straight and trying to find a job? How daft was that, to give the clock to your mum and the candlesticks to your girlfriend? Why don't you give going straight a try?'

'If Chelsea forgives me, I might, but not if I go down. She'll dump me for sure if that happens,' he stated mournfully.

'You've not been in court before, even though you're

218

on file. I think you might get off with a suspended sentence,' Falconer informed him, truthfully.

'Bonzer! Maybe she'll give me another chance. I've gotta tell her because of them candlesticks. What a bummer. I shoulda hocked them when I had the chance.'

'We'd have got our hands on them sooner or later. They're on a list that we circulate to all antique and second-hand dealers, as well as pawnbrokers.'

'I couldn't have got away with it, then.'

'Very unlikely. Take your lumps and try to keep your hands to yourself.'

When he had finished, he found that Tomlinson had got the gist of the case, and was eager to accompany them on their afternoon visit. As he put it, 'I'm not officially on the strength yet, but I might be of use.'

'Fair enough, but we can't go in my car. I've only got a two-seater, and I'm much too scared to go in Carmichael's. It's only the rust and elastic bands that hold it together.

This was greeted by an indignant, 'Sir!' and a counter-offer from the new DC.

'We could go in mine. It's not brand new, but I keep it running sweet. It's an old Merc, and they just go on and on. And it's immaculate inside, as well as out and under the bonnet – promise you.'

'Thank you, Tomlinson. I think we'll take you up on that, and you can give us your thoughts on the case as we progress.'

By the time they got to Daffodil Cottage, Carmichael and Tomlinson were on first-name terms, and seemed to be getting on like the proverbial house on fire. 'I think you'd better stay outside on this one,' suggested Falconer. 'It's difficult enough getting two of us into one of these tiny cottages, especially with the size that Carmichael is, but I don't think we'll be very long, then we can introduce you to Rev. Florrie. She's a very good woman.'

Meanwhile, Elodie Sutherland was seething with anger at the visit she had received that morning. Although she knew she had done something to the public good, she had not liked the sergeant rummaging through her kitchen cupboards, nor the inspector noticing her mother's incontinence. There was something she needed to do which couldn't wait any longer, but she needed to get something of her late father's first. And, of course, make a nice hot milky drink for Mummy.

Rev. Florrie was having a cup of afternoon tea after a hectic morning and early afternoon when she heard the knock on her door. Opening it, she found Elodie Sutherland on her doorstep and immediately invited her in to join her at the kitchen table. 'Just go on through, and I'll be with you in a second, Miss Sutherland,' she said.

'Please call me Elodie,' replied the imposing figure, and strode off down the hall. Rev. Florrie popped into the downstairs cloakroom briefly, then went on into the kitchen to make another cup of tea.

'What can I do for you' There was a slight pause, then she managed to get the name out, 'Elodie?'

Miss Sutherland, with her hands entwined on the table top, said, 'It was about my confession the other day.'

'What about it?' asked the vicar, pouring milk into the dark brown liquid.

'I hadn't actually finished when we broke off,' replied the woman, looking down at her hands.

'I'm sorry about that. Do you want to go back to the church, or will here do?' Florrie put her mug in front of her and sat down opposite.

'Here would be fine. It's very kind of you to take the time.'

'Do I need to robe up or anything?'

'You're fine just how you are.'

'Shall we make a start then?'

'It was about the murders,' began Elodie Sutherland,

beginning to ferret around in her capacious handbag.

'You said you'd killed the three victims with your evil thoughts?'

'I did but, if you'd given me more time, I would have told you that I turned those thoughts into actions,' she said, suddenly putting her handbag on the floor and returning her hands to the table top holding an old service revolver.

Rev. Florrie shied away in fear at the sight of the weapon and began to bluster. 'Don't worry. I'm sure we can get matters sorted without recourse to violence.'

'We can't and you know it. I'm going to tell you how and why I did what I did, but afterwards I'm going to have to kill you too.'

'Must you?' It was a lame plea, and received no real consideration.

'Of course I must. But I must confess first to receive absolution,' stated Miss Sutherland, as if it were the most obvious thing in the world, to seek absolution from someone of the cloth, then murder them.

Rev. Florrie risked a glance at her watch and noted that it was only three fifteen, and the two detectives were unlikely to turn up before half past – maybe not until four o'clock. She had got to keep this woman talking to save her own life. 'Tell me all about it. God's love and forgiveness are infinite.' Better make it sound good, or the Sutherland woman might go off the deep end.

'Well, firstly, I wanted to be head chorister. God told me that I should have the honour. I knew that old Albert was in that position because of his age, and I was next in line. The only thing I could do to remove him was to do away with him. I've been waiting for years for him to "kick the bucket", to use the vernacular, and he just went on and on, never once being ill or threatening to be engulfed by some dreadful disease.

'God kept on at me to do something about it, and I had to listen. I'd got to the point where I couldn't wait any longer, so I hid in the choir vestry and waited until everyone else had gone, sneaking into the vestry just behind the stalls. Old Albert was still sitting leafing through his hymn book when I crept out. It was so easy, reaching over and grabbing him by his scrawny neck and twisting until he went limp and stopped croaking and scrabbling at my hands. He always bit his nails, though, so I didn't get any scratches, fortunately. He had no idea who was doing it to him.

'I also saw Rev. Monaghan on his way to visit his floozy when I sneaked out, and made my way stealthily home. I made an anonymous call about that, hoping that they would think he'd done it.

'I kept on thinking, though, about being choir mistress, because now God had decided that that was how he wanted me to serve the church. I'd like that even more, so I decided that Mrs Pooley had to go as well. If I could get my hands on that position, I might be able to wangle the position of organist, if I could think of something to do about Willard Scardifield, but things didn't go as I'd planned.

'I hung around after service, then crept back into the church. Mrs Pooley was lost in her playing, and the noise disguised my approach. I'd hidden in the vestry again, and I found an old misericord under the sink in there. I thought I could hit her with sufficient force to knock her out, so I picked it up.

'She went straight down onto the organ's manuals, and the noise was terrific, so I pulled her head back. At that point, I heard God's voice in my head again, so I started looking at the copy of the hymnal she had on the music stand and, by chance, I put my hand in my pocket. I had been thinking of finishing her off as I killed old Albert, but my hand chanced across a clothes peg.

'I always carry one with me, because of something I learnt years ago in the Mothers' Union. About you

222

suddenly finding you need a clipboard. If you have a piece of cardboard and a clothes peg, they make for an instant board on which to take notes.

'I took the clip out of my pocket and fastened it on her nose, then I took the hymnal and began tearing pages out of it and shoving them into her mouth. She'd had both the positions I had coveted – oh, don't forget to take that into account: after all, covetousness is breaking one of the Ten Commandments. Oh, how I hated her at that moment.

'And then it all backfired a bit when Thea Scardifield was asked to take choir practice. My mind didn't stop there, though. I wanted to administer the host during communion, and the only one who did that in our church was Silas Slater, and he had to go next. If I manage to get the chance to study, I'd like to do a degree in theology and become a vicar myself. I'd love to be ordained.

'You do understand that it was God's voice telling me to do all this? I was only acting on instructions from on high. He often talks to me, and I, but a mere mortal, cannot help but do his bidding.

'Anyway, on the Sunday when I killed Silas, I was waiting round the side of the church for him to arrive …'

Millie Foster had been very honest about her relationship with Rev. Monaghan, and had given times for their recent meeting, giving him an alibi at least for Albert Burton's death and, although she wasn't quite sure of the times of his arrival and departure, for the murder of Yvonne Pooley as well. She made no fuss about confessing the details of their liaison, feeling sure that she was the gossip of the village anyway. They were not there long and, as Falconer and Carmichael got back into the car, Carmichael suddenly made a noise like a startled ostrich, to which Falconer responded with, 'Whatever's up, Sergeant. Surely you can't be hungry again already?'

'I've just thought of something, sir. You know that thuriberly thingy that Silas was hit with?'

'Of course.'

'And you said it wouldn't have been heavy enough?'

'So, you've twigged have you?'

'That the murderer probably loaded it with a stone?'

'Yes. And where have you come across a stone, recently, that seemed to be very out of place?'

'In that dried-up old stick's kitchen cupboard.'

'Top marks. So, we'll pay her another visit after we've been to Rev. Florrie's. No rush. She's not going anywhere.'

'When he arrived,' continued Elodie Sutherland, as Florrie nervously eyed up the gun in her hands, 'I gave him enough time to get into the vestry, then I crept in and hid behind the female choir stalls. I had to time this one just right, to allow him time to robe up and get the charcoal going before he hung up the thurible on the nail outside the vestry, then wait for him to go back in to wait for the vicar – you, that is, so that I could flush him out again.'

At that moment the doorbell rang, but Florrie was kept in her chair and silenced by the gun being pointed at her. The ring sounded again, then a third time, this time accompanied by a flourish on the knocker. 'You just stay where you are. They'll soon get tired of trying and go away,' said Elodie between gritted teeth. Her nerves were showing, and she put the gun back down on the table, still held in one hand, as she had begun to tremble.

There came no more noise from the front door, and she made as if to continue her 'confession' when, suddenly, the back door flew open, revealing the form of Rev. Monaghan. Elodie Sutherland sprang to her feet, brandishing the weapon at him.

Rev. Monaghan looked aghast at what confronted him, and let rip the loudest and longest fart that Florrie had ever heard. Elodie's nerve broke, and she began to laugh hysterically at this unexpected intrusion, and even more expected reaction.

Florrie seized her moment and came roaring round from the other side of the table to throw her full weight on to the woman's body, knocking her to the ground and dislodging the gun from her hand. She kicked it away from sheer reflex.

At that moment, there was another ring on the doorbell and, leaving the Rev. Monaghan staring open-mouthed at the scene before him, and Elodie Sutherland laughing helplessly on the floor, she went to answer the summons. It was twenty-five past three.

'Good afternoon, Inspector Falconer, Sergeant Carmichael. Come on in,' she said through chattering teeth, not even noticing that there was a third officer with them. 'We have a bit of a situation here that I think needs your professional attention.'

She led them into the kitchen and said, 'There is your murderer on the floor. She confessed all to me. And I'm sure you know Rev. Monaghan, who burst in in the nick of time. He probably saved my life, but in a very novel way.'

Tomlinson took a pair of gloves from his pocket, and an evidence bag, and took charge of the gun. 'Perhaps you'd like to make introductions, sir,' he asked, turning to the inspector.

'Where is your mother, Miss Sutherland?' he asked, before complying. 'Is she at home on her own?'

'I certainly left her there, but she's probably gone sleepy-byes by now,' replied Elodie, with a sly grin on her face.

Falconer twigged immediately, and barked out, 'Have you drugged her? Or something worse?'

'I just gave her a nice hot milky drink, and she should be out of it by now.'

'Get an ambulance, Carmichael, call for back-up and alert Social Services. If she recovers, the old lady is going to need a nursing home place. Her daughter certainly won't be caring for her any more. Can I ask you to stay to make a statement, Rev. Monaghan?'

'I'd rather not, if you don't mind,' replied the vicar. 'I seem to have had an embarrassing accident.'

'Let him come into the station later, Inspector,' pleaded Florrie on his behalf, having a jolly good idea what the accident was, and not wanting to entertain its presence in her kitchen any longer.

Chapter Nineteen

Still Tuesday Afternoon

When a weeping Elodie Sutherland had been taken away, and they had received confirmation that the ambulance had collected her mother, drugged, but not yet dead, the four of them sat round Florrie's kitchen table for her to tell the three detectives exactly what had happened.

'... But she never finished telling me what happened with Silas Slater,' she finished.

'I think we can help you there, Florrie. You said she was hiding in the church, waiting. What we presume she was waiting for was for Silas to come out of the vestry. In the meantime, she had taken the thurible and inserted a heavy stone inside it. When he came back into the body of the church, she swung it and cracked him on the temple – more a lucky shot than anything else, then she took out the stone to take it home, and replaced the thurible back on the nail where it hung.

'The stone, she rinsed off, and hid in a kitchen cupboard, where Carmichael here stumbled across it by accident while making a cup of tea there. No, don't ask,' he said, as Florrie opened her mouth to enquire what on earth the sergeant was doing making tea in the Sutherlands' kitchen.

'If she'd thought to have thrown it into the garden, the chances were we would never have found it. Maybe her mother distracted her, and she just put it there out of sight, forgetting what she had done after she had attended to her mother. That's just speculation but no doubt she will tell us when we interview her. There's no point in her denying anything when she has confessed all to you.

'And it makes sense that it was she who made the anonymous phone call after catching a glimpse of Rev. Monaghan after the first murder. It was a great red herring, and the gentleman only cooperated reluctantly, although his girlfriend was a lot more forthcoming.'

'He's a really obnoxious man. I suppose this business of him playing away will all come out now that the case is solved,' said Rev. Florrie.

'I suspect that it might make it into the press in quite a big way,' replied Falconer with a twinkle in his eye. 'That should make the bishop sit up and take notice.'

Florrie clapped her hands with glee. 'I hope that means that he'll be moved to another living. Ooh, fingers crossed. We could have a secret service of thanksgiving on our lucky deliverance from his ever-wandering hands his BO, halitosis – and his fragrant flatulence.'

'Are you feeling all right? You've had a nasty shock, finding yourself in danger like that,' enquired the inspector. He thought she was talking rather wildly.

'I shall go round to Mrs Mundy's and beg a cup of tea and a shoulder to cry on. She'll be delighted to find out exactly what has happened, and be the first one with the news.'

'Tell her not to spread it too far just yet. It's early days.'

Back in the station, Falconer had contacted Roberts on his mobile phone, and was explaining to him that they had recovered the candlesticks from the robbery at his house. 'No, we can't post them up to you. You know that they have to stay with us as evidence until after the young man's trial.' 'No, of course we didn't get your cash back. How on earth could we identify it? Of course we'll inform you for the date, so that you can be here if you want to come. You've got what now? Shingles? Roberts, you're a one-off.'

As he hung up, he turned round and announced to both Carmichael and Tomlinson, 'Roberts has got shingles now. Talk about *acting* as you mean to go on. I feel sorry for his new colleagues. It'll be bubonic plague next, if I know our ex-DC.'

'I've just taken a call from the hospital,' declared the sergeant, 'to say that Mrs Sutherland has regained consciousness, and that they have found her a place in a nursing home for when she's discharged. They've identified that she was drugged with sleeping tablets, and her daughter's GP has confirmed that she had been prescribed them for the "voice in her head". He had been getting quite worried about her, but was appalled at what she'd done to her mother.

'You wait till he hears about what else she's been up to.' Carmichael said to him. 'He should definitely have referred her for mental assessment earlier, if she'd been hearing voices, although it seems that she thought it was God's voice telling her what to do.'

'Just the daughter to deal with, now, then. Let's get on with it. Tomlinson, we'll be back as soon as we can, then I'll go through the area map with you and tell you a bit about the dodgier areas.'

When Falconer got down to the interview room, the breath was knocked out of his body to see his former sort-of girlfriend, Hortense 'Honey' Dubois, the force's mental health consultant, sitting with his suspect. They had parted on bad terms some months ago, and he was speechless with embarrassment but also a strange warm feeling that spread from his middle outwards.

'Good afternoon, Inspector Falconer,' she said, her soft voice making the hairs on the back of his neck stand on end. 'I hope you're keeping well.' She smiled.

'Doctor Dubois. How nice to see you again,' he replied, his voice husky with emotion. Why was he feeling so turbulent emotionally? She had been far from faithful to him, and he had vowed never to have anything to do with her again, yet here was this same old longing that he used to feel.

'Miss Sutherland would simply like to make a statement. She denies nothing, claiming that God told her to do it, so that she could serve him better.'

'You have spoken to her?'

'Yes, and I should like a word with you after you have conducted your interview.'

Falconer put on the double tape and spoke the necessary headers, his voice not quite steady. Elodie Sutherland told her story without falter, denying nothing about the murders, adding that she had to obey the instructions she had heard in her head in order to serve the Lord better. She needed no questioning, but set off on her narrative, now restored from her near-collapse at being arrested to an almost triumphant narrative.

'I heard the voice of the Lord,' she began, 'and he was telling me that he wanted me to serve my church in a fuller way. He said that I should lead the church's musical worship by taking over as head chorister, and that I should do that by disposing of Albert Burton who was too old and should be dispatched to his maker, as his time was past.

'Breaking his neck was no trouble to me as I had done a self-defence course in Market Darley when Father died, it not being appropriate that two defenceless women should live together without some sort of protection. I liked it so much that I did a further course in unarmed combat, and lifting Mother all around the house has done wonders for my muscles. I also train with dumb-bells, which you will no doubt find when you go through my home.'

At this point, Carmichael stared at Falconer, who

merely nodded his head to confirm that he had already ascertained that.

'This was not enough, however, as the voice in my head returned, and told me I should lead the choir as its mistress' – she blushed as she thought of the more common meaning of the word. 'That meant that I had to do something about Yvonne Pooley. I must admit I've never liked the woman, and was not upset to be guided to dispose of her: she was such an arrogant woman. I thought I dealt with her in a fitting way, as I had done with old Mr Burton by seeing him off in his beloved choir stalls.

'Woe to him who does not obey the commands of the Lord.' At this point there was definitely a challenging spark in her eyes, and Falconer momentarily looked away, so disconcerted was he. He had never come across a case of genuine religious mania before, although he wasn't sure he confronted one now.

'The Lord my God wanted me to serve the body of his only son ever to walk this earth by handing out the body of Christ at communion, and I had to do as I was bidden. Silas Slater was the only one who stood between me and God's mission for me in his church, and so I went there on the Sunday to do just that.'

'Did you intend to kill the Reverend Feldman as well?

'Of course. How else could I have answered my higher calling, to lead the flock of Ford Hollow?'

'Is that why you didn't object to there being a woman vicar in the parish? You strike me as someone who would have had quite a negative reaction to that, being so traditional.'

'How could I possibly object when I wanted her role eventually?' she replied with a thin-lipped smile.

'I see.' Falconer almost did understand, but was still appalled at what the woman had deemed fit to do in response to her calling from her Lord. After all, what about *Thou shalt not kill*?

'How is my mother?' she suddenly asked, changing the subject. 'I can't seem to remember.' Elodie's face clouded at these remarks, and she suddenly looked uncertain of herself.

'Mrs Sutherland is in hospital, but will be transferred to a nursing home as soon as she is fit,' Miss Sutherland.

'Why is she in hospital? I don't understand.'

'Because before you went to the vicarage, you gave her a milky drink with an overdose of sleeping tablets in it.'

'I couldn't have done. I would remember.' She was now distraught, and tears glinted in her eyes. 'I would never do that to Mummy.'

'I'm afraid that you have been under great stress looking after her, and may suffer a bit of traumatic amnesia because of what occurred when you reached the vicarage,' Falconer replied, determined not to soft-soap her about what she had done. He had managed to ignore Honey's presence, and was getting on with this interview as he would have done any other.

'Would you be prepared to sign a statement about these three deaths, and your intentions towards Rev. Feldman?'

'I would, just not the bit about Mummy. I can't have done that. And you must remember that, as far as the deaths are concerned, I did everything at the Lord's behest.'

That was fine with the inspector. There would prove to be no other fingerprints on the cup, saucepan, and milk bottle than Miss Sutherland's and her mother's, and she would be unable to deny the charge of attempted murder.

When she was returned to her cell, begging to be allowed to visit her mother, showing no memory whatsoever of this act, Honey went to look out of the window while Falconer and Carmichael removed the tapes from the machine and gathered their papers together. 'And you can give me my cap back at the end of today,' Falconer suddenly said, apropos of nothing. 'Either those henna tattoos have started to fade or your hair must have grown enough for it to look as if you've just had a very short haircut.'

'Aw, sir,' said Carmichael, with real regret in his voice.

'And that's why. I don't want you to become too attached to it, because I really like it myself. It fits just right for when I've got the top off the car and the wind in my hair. You can leave it in the office when you knock off this evening.'

Carmichael suddenly unloaded what was on his mind. 'You looked as if you already knew about her courses in self-defence and unarmed combat.'

'That's because I did. With everything that's happened, I forgot to tell you that I phoned the college earlier on and got the information from them. I had the feeling that whoever committed the first murder would have to have fairly strong hands and, after you finding that stone in Sutherland's kitchen cupboard, and a stray comment she made about self-defence, I made enquiries, as I couldn't think how else a woman of her age could have done it.'

Carmichael made his way off back to the office, and Falconer suddenly found himself alone with Honey, clearing his throat with embarrassment. 'I'm sorry if I seemed harsh with you, but I cannot condone unfaithfulness,' he croaked, rather unfairly (if not by his meticulous standards), the unsettled feeling he had felt when he first saw her, returning.

'I'm sorry that my judgement was so clouded that I did something terrible without thinking. Can you ever forgive me?'

Falconer stood in front of her silently for a full minute, then asked, 'Is she fit to plead?'

'At the moment, I'm not sure. I will have to see her again.'

'As will I.'

There was another moment of awkward silence, before

Honey spoke again. 'Can we not even go for a drink together for old times' sake?' she asked, slipping her hand gently into his.

Drawing his hand away, he said, 'I have a, sort of, girlfriend now.'

'It's only a drink,' said Honey, slipping her hand back into his and smiling up at him. 'Just for auld lang syne.'

Life in Ford Hollow slipped back into its previous gentle rut. Rev. Florrie made inroads in recruiting new members for the choir, and there was a late parish picnic, for which the sun still shone, and it was warm, if one was sitting in it.

The planning permission for the building of new houses was denied due to damage to the environment and lack of amenities nearby, and the state of the economy made it unlikely that it would ever have been passed on to a builder in the foreseeable future. Landbank Ltd, therefore, had to declare itself bankrupt, and the four men went their separate ways to lick their wounds in private.

Rev. Monaghan was, indeed, moved on by the bishop who made it patently clear that it was only because he had been found out that he had had to take action. He was moved to a parish and stripped of his position as head of a team ministry, having been told to behave himself in future, and look after his wife, who was soon expected to give birth.

Elodie Sutherland had been deemed unfit to plead, but had been allowed an accompanied visit to the nursing home to see her mother.

Inspector Falconer, meanwhile, lived in a state of emotional confusion, unable to sort out exactly how he felt about Honey, and feeling extremely guilty about Heather Antrobus, his current casual girlfriend. He had a lot of thinking to do, and could not get out of his mind the softness of the skin of Honey's hand, and the slenderness of it. Her coffee-coloured skin appeared often in his dreams, and he had not a clue what to do about the way he felt.

His only solace and comfort at the moment was to be found from his cats, who loved him because he looked after them, and because he could open a can.

THE END

Other titles by Andrea Frazer

For more information about **Andrea Frazer**
and other **Accent Press** titles
please visit

www.accentpress.co.uk